Books by Ignazio Silone

Fontamara

FONT

AMARA

by Ignazio Silone

Translated from the Italian

by Harvey Fergusson II

Foreword by Malcolm Cowley

New York   Atheneum Publishers   1960

Foreword   BY MALCOLM COWLEY

Books, like people, die; only a few of them have a persistent life. Among all the novels of the 1930's, in all the Western literatures, that were praised for being "proletarian" or "revolutionary," exactly three have survived into the present era without losing their force. One French, one American, and one Italian, they are curiously alike and not alike. *Man's Fate*, by André Malraux, is a psychological novel of violent action, one that tells how it feels to commit a political murder, how it feels to organize a workers' uprising, how it feels to have the uprising betrayed and to die with hundreds of workers in a mass execution. The workers are always there, but in the background, since Malraux's concern is with the leaders—especially Kyo—as models of revolutionary consciousness. In *The Grapes of Wrath* leaders are incidental, being created by the needs of a suffering mass that is represented, not led, by the Joad family. The mass is Steinbeck's hero. His novel survives—it even grows in retrospect without much help from critics—as a legend of dispossessed farmers embarked on a blind and apparently hopeless pilgrimage.

Fontamara is also a legend of families dispossessed from the soil, but one that belongs to a different tradition. What the novel suggests—or rather what it suggested in the original version—is the group of medieval fables that deal with peasants and the Devil. The peasants are always preposterously stupid and ignorant, but shrewd in their own fashion. The Devil is full of artifice, and sometimes he is helped by a priest, but he is sure to be defeated in the end. *Fontamara* couldn't have that happy ending because it was written in 1930, when Mussolini had crushed every movement toward popular revolt. The author himself, broken in health and harried into exile, had to tell a story in which the Devil—this time incarnated as a Fascist official, the Promoter—robbed the peasants of their water, killed the boldest of them, and scattered the others into the hills. As in the other novels, however, there was the hint of an apocalypse to come. Some day, Silone seemed to imply, the peasants would unite with their fellow sufferers in Italian cities and would triumph over landlords, priests, the Fascist militia, and Satan himself.

Among those few lasting novels of a revolutionary era, *Fontamara* is the only one to have been revised after the Second World War. Silone in exile had lost his lingering faith in Communism and indeed in every revolution directed by a bureaucratic party. He had greatly developed a feeling always latent in his work, a primitive Christian sense of communion and self-immolation. When he went back to Rome after the war and prepared a new edition of *Fontamara*—fifteen years after the original version, which had never been published in Italy—he repainted the whole canvas, as he says, in the effort to express his new conception of human destiny.

One is surprised to find that the changes he made are somewhat less extensive than he suggests in his prefatory note. The novel begins and ends as before. Chiefly his revisions consist in omitting several passages—among them one long episode—and in telling us more about the life of Berardo Viola, but still their effect is decisive. In the new version, as translated by Harvey Fergusson II, the community recedes into the background—much as in *Man's Fate*—and Berardo comes forward as the hero and dying god. We still have the sense of hearing a medieval legend, rough-hewn and angular, reduced to its essential outlines as if by generations of storytellers in the village marketplace, but it is no longer a *fabliau* about peasants and the Devil. Instead it becomes a golden legend about Christ reborn, tempted in the wilderness, and crucified in Jerusalem—or is Berardo rather John Baptist, who prophesies the coming of the Solitary Stranger?

There are some changes that readers of the earlier version will regret. Silone was right to omit most of the social or statistical information with which he had sprinkled the narrative; it seemed necessary in 1930, when he was fighting Mussolini with facts. Now the facts would be purely historical. On the other hand, one misses the gross peasant humor that was expressed in the little tale of Roscetta, the she-goat who liked young men, as well as in the long interpolated story about Peppino Goriano, the beggar and pimp who became a Fascist hero. I suppose the author feared that both episodes would diminish the force of what has become a unified and tragic narrative.

Losing some of its humor, the new version gains in somber intensity, being stripped of everything inessential so as to reveal the permanent themes of poverty, brotherly love, and sacrifice. Because of this changed emphasis, the question asked by a peasant at the end of the book—"What can we do?"—takes on a broader meaning. In the earlier version one felt that the peasant was unconsciously echoing Lenin's "What is to be done?" Any reader might assume, rightly or wrongly, that Silone's answer would be a simple one: the peasants should follow Lenin's advice by joining forces with the factory workers under Communist leadership. But the question has now become moral rather than political, and Silone himself, not knowing the answer, is humbly asking, "In this human situation, which always seems hopeless, what can we, what shall we, do to enhance the dignity of Man?"

A Note on the Revision of FONTAMARA

The readers of the present version of FONTAMARA who might be curious enough to compare it with the first translation, which appeared in 1934, would easily get the impression that it was a work which was, if not entirely new, certainly very different. To these readers I must explain that this impression comes not only from the differing personalities of the translators (although both know that the translator's job in literature is sometimes as important and decisive as the performer's in music) but also from another source, which really comes first: the notable diversity of the Italian texts on which the two translations were based.

The better to explain the origin and meaning of the changes which I made in FONTAMARA on the occasion of its first printing in Italy after the fall of Fascism, I must say something more general on the relationship between myself and my books. I agree entirely with what Hugo von Hofmannsthal said about writers: that they are the sort of men for whom writing is more difficult than for others. The cause of this is obvious to me whenever I am ready to finish a book. Every time, this process seems to me an arbitrary, painful and unnatural act (or at least against my nature). Therefore, because I feel myself bound up in a most intimate way with the story, it happens that I continue to think and dream about it, and in this way the book continues to live, grow and change within me even when it is already in a bookseller's window.

In addition to this state of mind there is a special reason for change in the case of FONTAMARA. As is indicated at the end of the introduction, I wrote this book in 1930 when I was in exile in Switzerland, at Davos, a small place known throughout the world for its sanitaria and ski runs. Since I was alone there—a stranger with an alias to evade the efforts of the Fascist police to find me—writing became my only means of defense against despair. And since it did not appear that I had long to live, I wrote hurriedly, with unspeakable affliction and anxiety, to set up as best I could that village into which I put the quintessence of myself and my native heath so that I could at least die among my own people.

Later, for good or for ill, life won out, and among its unforeseen surprises it came about that that desperate refuge of the writer became my secret dwelling place for the rest of a long exile. In fact, it would be wrong to believe that between that book of mine and its successors there had been any definite break. The stories of Pietro Spina in BREAD AND WINE, of Rocco in A HANDFUL OF BLACKBERRIES, and of Andrea in THE SECRET OF LUCA are related to the Stranger who makes his first appearance at the end of FONTAMARA. What is more, if it were in my power to change the mercantile laws of literary society, I could easily spin out my existence writing and rewriting the same story in the hope that I might end up understanding it and making it clear to others, just as in the Middle Ages there were monks whose entire lives were devoted to painting the face of Christ over and over again.

Therefore, when I was able several years later to return to my country and had to concern myself with the first printing of FONTAMARA by an Italian publisher, my surprise at rereading the text was far from small. Contrary to what might be believed, my concern was not due at all to the contrast between my book and the natural reality which I had before my eyes, but to the contrast between the story of 1930 and its development in me since then during all those years in which I had continued to live in it.

To take up the comparison with the painter, I painted the picture all over again from top to bottom, using the old canvas and frame.

Ignazio Silone

Rome, 1959

Fontamara

The strange events that I am about to set down took place last summer at Fontamara.

I have given this name to an old and obscure village of poor farmers situated near Marsica, north of what used to be Lake Fucino, in a valley halfway between the hills and the mountains. Afterward I found out that this name, sometimes with slight variations, belongs to other towns of southern Italy, and—a fact of greater importance—that the strange events so faithfully recorded in this book have occurred in several places, though not in the same order nor at the same time. But these did not seem to be valid reasons for concealing the truth. Even some of the names—such as Maria, Francesco, Giovanni, Lucia, Antonio and many others—are quite common. But then the really important events in one's life—birth, death, love, suffering—are also common to us all. Nevertheless, men never get tired of telling each other about them.

Fontamara is therefore similar in many respects to any other not-very-accessible south Italian village that lies between the plains and the mountains, away from the traffic, and hence is a little more backward, miserable and abandoned than its neighbors. But Fontamara has its own particular qualities.

In the same way, all poor farmers are alike in every country. They are men who cause the earth to bear fruit; they suffer from hunger; and whether they are called fellahs, coolies, peons, muzhiks or *cafoni*, they form their own nation, their own race and their own church all over the world, even though no two are exactly alike.

If you go up from the plain of Fucino to Fontamara, you see the village laid out on the side of a gray mountain, as bare and lifeless as a flight of stone steps. Most of the doors and windows of the houses are clearly visible from the plain: a hundred little huts almost all on the same level—irregular, unformed, blackened by time and worn down by wind, rain and fire, with their roofs poorly covered by all sorts of tiles and scrap lumber.

Most of these hovels have only one opening, which serves as door, window and chimney. In the dry-walled interiors, which seldom possess a floor, the men, women and children, and their goats, chickens, pigs and donkeys live, sleep, eat and reproduce, sometimes all in the same corner. The exceptions are about ten houses belonging to small landowners and an old uninhabited palace that is almost in ruins. The upper part of Fontamara is dominated by the church with its tower and the terraced square, reached by a steep road that goes through the entire village and is the only one over which carts can pass. On either side of it are narrow little alleys, mostly consisting of rugged short steps over which the roofs nearly touch and barely let in the light of day.

To an observer as far away as the fief of Fucino, the village looks like a herd of dark sheep, and the church tower like a shepherd. It is, in short, a village like so many others, but the universe to those who grow up there. Here all that is universal—birth and death, love and hate, jealousy and desperation—is carried on.

There would be nothing else to tell of Fontamara if the strange events that I am about to relate had not taken place. Here I passed the first twenty years of my life, but if these events had not taken place, I wouldn't know how to say anything more.

For twenty years I lived under the same sky, surrounded by the amphitheater of the mountains, which form an insurmountable barrier to the fief. For twenty years there was the same land, the same rain, the same snow, the same saints' days, the same food, the same anguish, the same pain, and the same misery—the misery received from the fathers, who had inherited it from the grandfathers, and against which honest hard work has never been good for anything. The cruelest injustices there were so old that they took their places among the natural phenomena like the wind, the rain and the snow. The life of the men, the beasts and the land seemed fixed in an inflexible circle, hemmed in by the position of the mountains and the passage of time, as if condemned by nature to life imprisonment.

First would come the planting, then the fumigating, then the reaping, then the gathering of the grapes. And then? And then all over again from the beginning. The planting, the weeding, the pruning, the fumigating, the reaping, and the gathering of the grapes. Always the same song with the same chorus. Always. The years passed on and accumulated. The young became old and the old people died. And the planting, the weeding, the fumigating, the reaping and the gathering went on. And then what? It started from the beginning all over again. Every year was like the one before; every season like the one before; every generation like the one before. No one at Fontamara had ever thought that this way of life could change.

There are only two rungs on the social ladder at Fontamara: that of the peasant, who is bound to the soil, and that of the small landowner, who stands a little higher. The artisans are also divided this way: those with a tiny shop or some rudimentary equipment are a little better off; the others are on the street. For several generations the peasants, the farm hands, the workers and the poorer artisans have struggled through privations and unheard-of sacrifices to rise from the lowest social level, but they rarely succeed. The salvation of the fortunate at Fontamara is marriage to a small landowner's daughter. But if you stop to think that there is land around Fontamara where only a ton of grain is harvested for a ton of seed sown, you can easily understand that so many fall from the position of small proprietor, gained with so much effort, to that of peasant.

(I know quite well that the term *peasant* in the current vocabulary of my part of the world, whether in the city or in the country, is now an offensive and scornful one. But I use it in this book in the certainty that when misery is no longer shameful in my village, it will become respectable and perhaps even honorable.)

The most fortunate of the peasants of Fontamara have a donkey and sometimes a mule. When autumn comes and they have with great difficulty paid up last year's debts, they must try to borrow the few potatoes, beans and onions, the little flour and corn that will keep them from starving in the winter. Most of their lives are burdened with a series of debts contracted to buy food and the exhausting work necessary to pay them off. When the harvest is exceptionally good and brings forth unforeseen gains, these gains serve as occasions for lawsuits. I must explain that in Fontamara there are no two families that aren't related. (In the mountains generally everyone ends up related to everyone else.) All the families, even the poorest ones, have interests to divide among themselves, and if there are no goods to share, they share their misery. Therefore at Fontamara there is no family without some suit pending. As is known, the suits die down in the lean years, but they become bitter as soon as there is money with which to pay the lawyer. And there are always the same suits, unending lawsuits that are passed on from generation to generation in interminable hearings, eternal expenses, in blind in-extinguishable bitterness—to establish the owner-ship of some thornbush grove. The grove may burn down, but the suit continues even more bitterly.

There never was any way out. Setting aside twenty soldi per month, or thirty, or even a hundred in summer, you could in those days save up about thirty lire by autumn. But they went quickly—for the interest on some loan, or to the lawyer, the priest or the druggist. And the whole process began once again the following spring: twenty, thirty, a hun-dred soldi per month. And then all over again from the beginning.

Everyone knows that many things change down below, at least in appearance, but nothing changes at Fontamara. The people of Fontamara watch the changes on the plain with neither interest nor under-standing. The soil on the mountains is insufficient, arid, and stony, and the climate unfavorable. The draining of Lake Fucino about eighty years ago was advantageous to the towns on the plain, but not to the ones in the mountains. For it caused a sig-nificant drop in temperature throughout Marsica, so that all the former crops were ruined. The old olive trees were entirely destroyed. The vineyards were often infected, and the grapes never com-pletely matured. To prevent their being frozen with the first snows, they had to be picked hurriedly at the end of October, and thus they gave a lemon-bitter wine. For the most part, the ones who harvest the grapes have to drink the wine.

This damage would have been largely compensated for by the cultivation of the extremely fertile land from the bottom of the lake if the valley of Fucino weren't under such a colonial regime. The great wealth annually harvested from there enriches a restricted circle of inhabitants, and the rest finds its way to the metropolis. In fact, it must be pointed out that, together with expanses of land in the Agro Romano and the Maremma, the thirty-five thousand acres of Fucino are the property of the so-called Princes Torlonia, who descended on Rome in the first years of the last century on the heels of a French regiment. But this is another story entirely. And perhaps after I have told this gloomy tale of the people of Fontamara, I will write an edifying life of the Torlognes, as they were first called, to console my readers. Reading this would surely be more amusing. The obscure story of the people of Fontamara is a monotonous *Via Crucis* of hungry and unsuccessful peasants who for generations have worked from dawn to sunset, sweating blood over a minute and sterile patch of dust. But the lot of the Torlognes has been the precise opposite. None of them has ever touched the earth, not even for amusement, and they own incredible expanses of it, a fat kingdom of tens of thousands of acres.

The Torlognes came to Rome in time of war and speculated on war, then they speculated on peace, then on the salt monopoly, then on the revolutions of 1848, on the war of 1859, on the Bourbons of the Neapolitan kingdom and on their ruin. Later they speculated on the House of Savoy, on democracy and on dictatorship. Thus they made millions without taking off their gloves. After 1860 a Torlogne succeeded in buying very cheaply the control of a Franco-Hispano-Neapolitan Company that had constructed the outlet for draining the lake and which was in trouble because of the collapse of the Bourbon regime. According to the company's charter, recognized by the King of Naples, the Torlognes were to have the benefit of the reclaimed land for ninety years. But in exchange for the political support he offered to the insecure Piedmontese dynasty, Torlogne received the land in perpetuity. He was given the title of duke and later of prince. In short, the Piedmontese dynasty gave him something that didn't belong to it. The people of Fontamara watched the spectacle going on down below and found it natural, even though it was new, because it was in harmony with other abuses. But in the mountains things went on as before.

At one time the people of the mountains could at least emigrate to America. Before the great war, even people from Fontamara tried their luck in Argentina and Brazil. But those who were able to return to Fontamara with some bank notes between their skin and their shirt soon lost their small savings on the sterile, arid lands of their native heath, and fell back into the former lethargy, keeping the memory of their life abroad as a lost paradise.

But last year there was a series of unforeseen and incomprehensible events that completely upset in Fontamara the life that had been stagnant from time immemorial. For several months no one bothered about what was going on, but finally an inkling of it began to leak out to other parts of Italy and even abroad, where, to my sorrow, I am obliged to take refuge. Thus Fontamara, which is on no map, became the theme of strange discussions and conjectures. I grew up in Fontamara, and in spite of an absence of several years, still felt I knew it well enough to suspect that the events that were supposed to have happened there were entirely fictitious and had been attributed to Fontamara because of the difficulty of checking up on so remote a village. I made several attempts to get direct information and failed. Nonetheless, not a day passed without my thinking about it and returning in my imagination to the countryside I knew so well, consumed by the desire to know the truth.

One day something quite unexpected happened. In the evening, when nostalgia is strongest, I was astonished to find three peasants—two men and a woman—nearly asleep on my doorstep, with their backs to the door. I realized at once that they were from Fontamara. At my arrival they got up and followed me inside, where I recognized their faces by the light of the lamp. The man was old, tall and thin, with an earthy face and greasy gray hair. With him were his wife and son. They came in and sat down. They started talking. (Then I recognized their voices too.)

The old man spoke first. Then his wife. Then the old man again. Then his wife. I am afraid I fell asleep while the woman was speaking, but, strange to say, without losing the gist of what she was talking about, almost as if her voice rose from the depths of my being. When dawn came and I woke up, the old man spoke once again.

What they told me is in this book.

And now two words of caution. To the foreigner, who will be the first to read it, the story will appear in strong contrast to the picturesque idea of southern Italy frequently found in literature. As some books have it, southern Italy is a very beautiful land, where farmers go off to work signing joyous songs to which the peasant girls in traditional costume respond, while the nearby woods resound with the song of birds.

But these marvelous things have never happened at Fontamara.

The people of Fontamara are dressed like the country poor all over the world. And there aren't any woods at Fontamara. The mountain is dry and bare like most of the Apennines. The birds are quite rare and very timid because they are mercilessly hunted. Nor are there any nightingales, there isn't even a word for them in the local dialect. The farmers don't sing, whether in groups or alone, even when they're drunk, let alone on their way to work. Instead of singing, they curse freely. They curse to express any strong emotion—joy, anger and even religious feeling. But there isn't much imagination in their cursing, and they swear by one or two local saints whom they know. They always curse with the same jaded exclamations.

The only one I knew at Fontamara during my adolescence who sang incessantly was a shoemaker. He sang only one song, which dated back to the first African war, and began:

> *You'll never get back,*
> *If you trust in a black,*
> *O Baldissera . . .*

Hearing this warning every day in the year from dawn to dusk from a voice that perceptibly aged with its owner made the children of Fontamara seriously fear that General Baldissera, whether through rashness, distraction or carelessness, would end up trusting in the blacks. Much later we learned that this had already happened before we were born.

The second word of caution is this: in what language should I tell this story?

Don't think for a moment that Italian is spoken at Fontamara. It is for us a language learned at school, like Latin, French or Esperanto. It is a foreign tongue for us, a dead language whose vocabulary and grammar have grown apart from our way of acting and expressing ourselves.

Naturally other southern peasants have spoken and written Italian before me, just as we put on shoes, collars and ties when we go to town. But you can tell at a glance how awkward we are. When it shapes our thoughts the Italian language can only mangle and cripple them, so that they appear to have been badly translated. And translation is never direct expression. If it is true that one should learn to think in a language before expressing oneself in it, the trials we go through to speak Italian evidently mean that we cannot really think in it. The Italian culture has always been school culture for us.

But since I have no other means of making myself understood (and self-expression for me is an absolute need), I wish to do my best to translate into the language I have learned what I want all the world to know—the truth about what happened at Fontamara.

Nevertheless, even if the language is borrowed, the way the story is told seems to me to be ours. It is an art of Fontamara. I learned it as a boy, seated on the threshold of my house or at the hearth during the long evenings or near the weaver, following the rhythm of the pedal, listening to the age-old tales.

There is no difference between this art of story-telling, this art of making words, lines, sentences

and images follow one another, of explaining something once without allusions or subtleties, calling
wine, wine, and bread, bread, and this ancient art
of weaving, this art of making threads and colors
follow one another in a neat, clear and orderly
fashion. First you see the stalk of the rose, then
the petal, then the crown; but we all know it's going
to be a rose from the beginning. This is why our
products look so crude and childish to the city people. But when did we ever try to sell them in the
city? Did we ever ask the townsmen to tell their
stories in our way? Never.

Therefore let everyone have the right to tell his
own story in his own way.

1.

On the first of June Fontamara was without electricity for the first time. On the second of June, the third of June, and the fourth of June Fontamara continued to do without electricity. It kept on like this for days and months, until Fontamara got used to moonlight again. It had taken about a hundred years to go from moonlight to olive oil to kerosene to electricity. In just one night the village went back to moonlight.

The young people don't know history but we old people do. In seventy years the only important things the Piedmontese had brought us were electric lights and cigarettes. Now they've taken back the lights, and as for the cigarettes, anyone who smokes them deserves to choke. A pipe has always been good enough for us.

Electric lights were as natural to us as moonlight; nobody paid for either. Nobody paid for several months. And what were we going to pay with? Just before the lights went out, the town clerk had come to distribute the usual monthly piece of paper with the unpaid amount on it (the only paper we had for domestic purposes). The last time he came, he barely escaped with his skin. They nearly shot him at the village boundary.

He was very careful. He came to Fontamara only when the men were at work and when there were just women and beasts at home. But you can never be careful enough. He was very affable. He handed out the papers with his silly little laugh, saying:

"Take it, for heaven's sake. There's always some use for a piece of paper in the family!"

But you can never be affable enough, either. A few days afterward a carter gave him to understand, not at Fontamara (he might never again have set foot in Fontamara), but in town, that the shot wasn't directed against him personally, against the person of Innocenzo La Legge, but rather against the tax. But if the shooting had been more accurate, it wouldn't have killed the tax, but him. If he never came back, no one would miss him. Nor was he ever inspired to propose a suit against the villagers of Fontamara.

"If we could confiscate the lice and sell them," he had once suggested, "it might be worth while suing them. But even if it were legal to confiscate lice, who'd buy them?"

The electricity was supposed to be cut off on the first of January, then on the first of March, then on the first of May. Then people began saying, "It'll never be cut off. The queen's probably against it. You'll see. It'll never be cut off." And on the first of June it was cut off.

The women and children at home were the last to realize what was happening. But as we came back from work—from the mill over the car road, through the mountains, from the cemetery, along the ditch from the sand cave, and from just about everywhere after day labor—as it gradually got dark and we saw the lights of the nearby villages come on and those of Fontamara turn pale, fade away and become confused with the rocks and ma- nure heaps, we understood what it was all about. (It was a surprise and yet no surprise.)

For the boys it was an excuse for a spree. Our boys don't have many chances like this, poor crea- tures, so they take advantage of all of them—when a motorcycle arrives, when donkeys mate, or when a chimney catches on fire.

When we got back to the village, we found General Baldissera swearing aloud in the middle of the street. In the summer he would repair shoes until late at night in front of his house and under the street lamp. Now he had no light. Rubbish was all around his little table and was getting con- fused with his chisels, nails, knives, pitch, string and sole leather. His bucket of dirty water was overturned, and he was swearing at the top of his lungs at the local saints. He asked us as we came from work whether it was a just thing that at his age and in his myopic condition he should lose the light from the street lamp and what Queen Mar- garet would think of such a situation.

It was hard to think what Queen Margaret would have thought.

Of course there were some women crying (no sense telling who they were), sitting on the ground in front of their houses, nursing their children or picking lice from their clothing, or cooking. They were crying as if someone were dead. They were bewailing the loss of the electric lights, as if their outlook were any darker without electricity.

Michele Zompa and I stopped at Marietta's place around the outdoor table and Losurdo came right afterward with the donkey he had brought to stud, and then came Ponzio Pilato with the fumigating pump on his back, and then came Ranocchia and Sciarappa, who had been pruning, then came Barletta, Venerdì Santo, Ciro Zironda, Papasisto and some others who had been to the sand cave. And we were all talking of the electric light, of new taxes, of old taxes, of communal taxes and of state taxes, repeating the same things because taxes never change. And without our being aware of it a stranger came up, a stranger with a bicycle. It was hard to say who he could be at that hour. He was definitely a stranger. And he wasn't the lightman. Nor a township man. Nor the policeman. He was a well-dressed lad, with a shaven and rosy little face and a great red mouth like a cat's. He held up his bike with one hand, and that hand was as small and sticky as a lizard's underbelly, and he had a large ring on his finger, like a monsignor. He had white spats on his shoes. He was altogether incomprehensible.

We didn't stop talking. It was obvious that this bird had come to tell us about some new tax. There was no doubt of that. There was no doubt that he had made the same useless trip and that his paper would end up in the same way Innocenzo La Legge's did. There was just one thing to clear up: what could they possibly put a new tax on? We were all thinking about it, and looked questioningly at one another. But nobody knew. Maybe a tax on moonlight?

Meanwhile the stranger had asked two or three times in his goatlike voice that he be shown the way to "the residence of the Widow of the Hero Sorcanera."

Marietta Sorcanera was there on the threshold of the inn, blocking the way with her swollen belly, the third or fourth since her husband had died in the war. Her husband had left her a silver medal along with the pension. But probably he didn't leave her the three or four pregnancies. On account of his glory, they said, she had got to know several important people after the war. They had taken her to Rome a couple of times and shown her to the authorities; they had fed her and paraded her along with hundreds of other widows, double step, under the windows of the palaces. But after she started getting pregnant, they didn't call her any more.

"Why don't you get married?" we kept asking her. "If you don't like being a widow, you could get married."

"If I get married," she answered, "I lose the

Hero's Widow's Pension. That's the way the law is. I have to be a widow."

And there were some men who agreed with her, but the women all hated her.

In other words, Marietta knew how to deal with important people. So she got the stranger to sit down at the table. He hauled several huge sheets of paper out of his pockets and put them on the table.

When we saw the papers we looked at one another and now we were sure. The papers were there, the tax papers. Now all we had to find out was what this new tax was about.

In fact, the stranger began talking. We caught on right away that he was a city fellow. We understood only a few of his very many words. Only we couldn't understand what sort of tax it was going to be. On moonlight maybe?

Meanwhile it had gotten late. We were there with our tools, hose, axes, pitchforks, shovels and Losurdo's donkey and sulphur pump. Some of us went off. We began hearing our wives from far away calling us back home. Venerdì Santo, Barletta and Papasisto went away. Sciarappa and Ranocchia listened to the stranger's rigmarole and went also. Losurdo wanted to stay, but his donkey, which was tired, persuaded him to go home.

Now there were just three of us and the city man. He kept right on talking. Every once in a while we looked at one another, but nobody understood what he was talking about. I mean nobody knew what the new tax was going to be on.

Finally he stopped talking. He turned to me because I was next to him, gave me a sheet of white paper and a pencil and said:

"Sign!"

Why should I sign? What did signing have to do with it? I hadn't caught ten words of what he had said. But why should I sign even if I had understood it? I just looked at him and didn't bother answering.

So he turned to the peasant next to me, gave him the pencil and paper and said:

"Sign! It's for your own good."

He didn't sign either. He just looked at him as if he were a tree or a rock. The stranger turned to the third peasant, gave him the paper and pencil and said:

"You begin. The rest of them will sign after you."

It was as if he had spoken to the wall. Nobody said anything. But if we didn't know what it was all about, why should we sign?

We just sat there and looked at him and he got furious. From the way he talked, I guess he said something bad about us. We waited for him to tell us about the new tax, but he was talking about something else. At one point he took a little whip he had with him and started waving it in my face.

"Talk! Talk!" he shouted. "Damned dog of a

worm! Why don't you talk? Why don't you want to sign?"

It takes more than that to make me lose my temper. We let him know we weren't idiots. We let him know that all this rigmarole hadn't convinced us that there wasn't to be a new tax.

"Come on!" I said. "Tell us about the new tax!"

He looked at me as if I had spoken Hebrew.

"We don't understand each other. We speak the same language and we don't understand each other," he said, discouraged.

This was true, but who doesn't know it? It's hard for a townsman and a peasant to understand each other. When he talked he was a townsman and he couldn't help but speak like one. But we were peasants. We understood things in our own way. It's occurred to me thousands of times in my life that peasants and townsmen are different. I was in the Argentine pampas when I was young, and there I talked with peasants of all races from Spanish to Indian, and we understood one another as if we all came from Fontamara. But we spoke with an Italian who came to us every Sunday from the consulate without understanding him. Sometimes we understood the exact opposite of what he said. On our farm there was a Portuguese deaf-mute and we understood each other even without speaking. But we didn't understand this Italian.

So I wasn't surprised when the stranger started up his speech again, trying to explain to us that there wasn't to be a new tax, that he had come to Fontamara for something else and that there wasn't anything more to pay at all.

Since it was late and had got dark, he lit some matches and showed us the pieces of paper, one by one. They were completely white. They were all white. There was a little something written at the top of each paper. The city man lit two more matches and showed us what was written there:

> The undersigned, in support of the above, sign their names of their own free will, voluntarily and with enthusiasm for the Cavaliere Pelino.

He assured us that he was the Cavaliere Pelino. "Don't you believe me?" he asked me.

"Maybe," I answered. "Everybody has a name."

Cavaliere Pelino had got the papers from his superiors. Identical papers had been taken to similar villages by his colleagues. In other words, it was nothing especially invented for Fontamara. It was for all the villages. It was a petition to the government, he told us. It had to have lots of signatures. The petition itself wasn't there; it had been written by his superiors. All he had to do was to collect signatures, and all the farmers had to do was to sign. Everybody had his duty.

"Understand?" he asked. "The time is over when the peasants were ignored and held in contempt. Now there is a new government that respects the peasants and wants to know their opinions. So sign, take advantage of the honor the government is doing you in sending a functionary to find out your opinions."

This argument made a certain impression on Marietta, while we were still a little bit suspicious. But meanwhile General Baldissera, who had heard the last explanation, had come up. He said firmly (you know how shoemakers are):

"If the honorable gentleman assures me that there's nothing to pay, I'll sign first."

He signed first, then I did. But now I can say that I was smart enough to sign the name of my dead father. You never know. Then Ponzio Pilato signed. (He was next to me.) Then Zompa. Then Marietta. And the others? How were we going to see them? It was impossible to go to their homes at that hour. Cavaliere Pelino solved the problem. We were to tell him the names of all the inhabitants of the village and he would write them down. That's what we did. There was only one argument and that was about Berardo Viola. We tried to make the Cavaliere Pelino understand that he wouldn't have signed in any event.

But his name was written down too.

"We'd better not tell him about it," suggested Marietta. "It would be more prudent."

The second sheet was already covered with names and the stranger had lit thirty or forty matches when he discovered something on the table. There was something on the table that disgusted him. But

there wasn't anything there. He lit a match and returned to stare fixedly at the table. He bent over
until he touched it with his nose. Then, pointing to
a spot on the table, he began shouting with his goatlike voice:

"What's this? Who's responsible for this nonsense? Who put it on the table?"

We could tell he wanted a fight. No one answered
him. General Baldissera prudently went away. The
stranger repeated the question four or five times
and lit three matches at once to shed more light
on the table. Finally we saw something on the
table, something moving. It wasn't as awful as all
that, but certainly there was something. Ponzio
Pilato got up first, bent over the table, looked at it
and said as he spat on the floor:

"It's not mine."

I explained to the townsman. "In this part of the
country only the sheep are branded. The other animals don't have to be."

But his ridiculous rage got worse.

Marietta bent over the table, looked at the insect
for a long time. By now it had already got to the
middle of the sheet with the names on it. She took
it in her hand and threw it into the middle of the
street. Then she said:

"That's strange. It looked like a new species.
It's darker and longer than the rest and it had a
cross on its back."

Michele Zompa, think of it, an old man like him,

was strangely impressed and turned to Marietta, almost screaming:

"What? Did it really have a cross on its back? Was it a new species?"

And he remembered a story (which we knew too, to tell the truth, but which we'd forgotten for the moment). All the species of animals were created in the beginning, right after man, even lice, as everybody knows. But God ordered that a new species of lice was to come after every great revolution. Then Zompa explained to us why he was so agitated.

"I had a dream last winter," he said. "I told the priest about it. But he told me not to tell anyone. Now that it has come true, if Marietta is right, I should certainly speak up."

We sat down around the table and Zompa continued.

"After the truce between the Pope and the government, the priest explained to us at Mass that there was to be a new era, even for the peasants. He said the Pope had received lots of grace from Christ, which the peasants need. That night I dreamed I saw the Pope talking with the Crucifix.

"The Crucifix said: 'To celebrate this truce it would be a good idea to give the land of Fucino to the peasants who cultivate it, the ones who are on the mountains without any land.' The Pope answered: 'But, Lord, the Prince Torlonia wouldn't have it. And the prince is a good Christian.' The

Crucifix said: 'It would at least be a good idea to exonerate the peasants from taxes.' The Pope answered: 'O Lord, the government couldn't think of it. And the government men are good Christians.' The Crucifix said: 'To celebrate the truce this year, let's send a good crop, especially to the peasants and small landowners.' The Pope answered: 'O Lord, if there is a good crop the prices will go down and that will ruin many great merchants. And these people are also worth attention, for they, too, are good Christians!'

"The Crucifix was very sad that He couldn't do anything for the peasants without hurting some good Christians.

"Then the Pope proposed a plan to the Crucifix. 'Lord, let's go there. Maybe we can do something for the peasants that won't get in the way of Prince Torlonia or the government or the rich.'

"On the night of the Conciliation Christ and the Pope came to Fucino and all the villages of Marsica. Christ went first with a great knapsack on His shoulders. The Pope came behind and had permission to take anything from the knapsack that might do the peasants some good. The two Heavenly Travelers saw the same thing in every village, and what else could they see? The peasants were lamenting, swearing, fighting, not knowing what to wear nor what to eat. So the Pope felt his heart breaking, and he took from the sack a cloud of lice of a new species and sent them to the houses of the poor, saying: 'Take them, O my beloved children, and scratch. Thus in your moments of temporal hate there will be something to take your thoughts away from sin.' "

This was Michele Zompa's dream. But everybody has his own way of interpreting dreams. Some play with dreams. Some read the future in them. I think dreams are to make you go to sleep. But Marietta Sorcanera, who was a devout women, didn't understand it in that way and began lamenting and sighing:

"It's true. Who would worry about our sins if the Pope didn't pray for us? Who else would save us from Hell?"

It was late and we wanted to go home. Just then, all of a sudden, I began feeling tired from my day's work. Why should I waste time with all this useless chatter?

But the Cavaliere Pelino misunderstood Marietta.

"You're making fun of me!" he screamed, waving the whip at Zompa and Marietta. "You're making fun of the authorities! You're making fun of the Church and the government!" And he said lots of other senseless things in this tone, and nobody understood him.

"The government will put you in your place!" he yelled. "The government will punish you. The authorities will take care of you!"

We were hoping that he would shut up after a

while and let us go home. But he kept talking.

"You don't know that if I were to report you, you would be condemned to at least ten years of imprisonment," he said directly to Zompa. "Don't you know that lots of people are serving out years for less than what you've just said? What sort of world do you live in? Don't you know who gives the orders? Don't you know who's boss?"

He was mad as a wet hen. Zompa kept sucking the end of his cold pipe. Then he spat on the floor and answered patiently.

"Look," he said. "A lot of things happen in the city. Something happens in the city at least once a day. They say a paper comes once a day and tells something that happened. At the end of the year how many things have happened? Hundreds and hundreds! Just think of it! How can a peasant, a poor peasant, a little worm, know all these things? He can't. The news is one thing. The boss is another. The news changes every day. The boss is always the same."

"And the hierarchies?" asked the stranger.

But we didn't know right away what that funny word meant. The city fellow had to repeat it several times.

Michele patiently explained our idea to him:

"God is at the head of everything. He commands in Heaven. Everybody knows that.

"Then comes Prince Torlonia, ruler of the earth.

"Then come his guards.

"Then come his guards' dogs.

"Then nothing.

"Then more nothing.

"Then still more nothing.

"Then come the peasants.

"That's all."

"But where do you put the authorities?" asked the still angrier stranger.

"The authorities are somewhere between the third and fourth places," said Ponzio Pilato, "according to their salaries. The fourth place, the dogs' place, is tremendous. We all know that."

Cavaliere Pelino had gotten up. He was trembling with rage. He told us: "I promise you, you'll hear from me soon!"

He leaped on his bicycle and went off.

But we didn't pay any attention to what he had said.

We said good night and went home. As I was feeling my way along the path of St. Anthony, I heard the tinkle of stones and broken glass. Right away I recognized the man at the end of the path because he was so tall. "What in Christ's name are you up to?" I yelled.

"What the hell good are lamps without any light?"

I went home to some cold soup, and Berardo went on breaking lamps.

2.

The next day at dawn Fontamara was in an uproar. Near the entrance to the village under a pile of stones there is a miserable, dirty little spring. A few paces farther on, the water disappears into a hole and comes out at the foot of the hill in the form of a brook. Before going down to the plain the stream turns several times. From it the peasants of Fontamara have always taken water for the few fields they possess, which are about the only wealth of the village. Every summer there are furious arguments over the division of the water. In the drought seasons they end up with stabbings. But this doesn't seem to get any more water.

In the summer season it is our custom for the men to get up at three thirty or four o'clock when it is still dark, drink a glass of wine, load up the donkey and silently go off to the plain. So that they will not lose time and get there when the sun is already high, they take their breakfast on the road. This breakfast is a crust of bread with an onion or a pepper or maybe some cheese.

Now the last of the farmers who on the second of June were going down the hill to work met a group of roadmen who had come down with picks and shovels to change the course of the water (so they said), to divert this miserable stream from the fields and meadows that it had bathed as long as anybody could remember, and send it on another course, causing it to pass by some vineyards and end up irrigating land that didn't belong to

Fontamara, but to a local landholder, don Carlo Magna. This man is from one of the oldest families of the countryside, a family that has nearly been ruined because of him. He is called don Carlo Magna because when someone asks for him the maid always answers, "Don Carlo? *Magna*—he's eating. If you wish, you may speak with the mistress." In that house it's his wife who runs things.

At first we thought the roadmen wanted to make fun of us. The city people (not all of them, but the usual crowd of loafers) never passed up a chance to make fun of our people. To tell you all the jokes they played on us would take a week. But just to give you the idea, here's the story of the priest and the donkey.

Fontamara hasn't had a curate for about forty years. The parish has too small an income to maintain one, and the church is open only for the great festivals when a priest comes from the city to read us the Bible and say a Mass. Two years ago we sent in a final plea to the bishop for a permanent priest. Nobody had any illusions, but the petition was sent. A few days later we were told that, contrary to our every expectation, the petition had been granted by the bishop and that we were to get ready for the arrival of our priest. Naturally we did our best. We are poor, but we know what should be done. The church was cleaned. The road that leads to Fontamara was done over and in some parts enlarged. At the entrance to the village there was a triumphal arch with curtains and flowers. The doors of the houses were adorned with green branches. Finally, on the day the priest was supposed to come, all the village went out to meet him. After a quarter of an hour's walk we saw a strange group coming to meet us. We didn't find any authorities or priests—just a lot of young squirts. We were following in a procession behind the banner of San Rocco, singing hymns and reciting the rosary. The older people were in front with General Baldissera, who was to make a little speech; the women and children went behind. When we got up to the city people, we lined up on the side of the road to greet the new priest. Only General Baldissera went ahead, waving his hat and yelling:

"Viva Gesù! Viva Maria! Viva la Chiesa!"

Just then the funny group from the city opened up and, urged on by kicks and stones, out ran the new curate—in the form of an old donkey covered with paper colored like priestly vestments.

It's not easy to forget jokes like that, even if the people in the city who have nothing to do think up new ones every day. That's why we thought the diversion of the stream was another joke. In fact, that would be the last straw if man's jokes were to change what was created by God, like the course of the sun, the wind and the water—things God has established. It was as if they had told us that donkeys were flying or that Torlonia was no longer a prince or that the peasants were no longer hungry;

in short, that God's eternal law wasn't God's eternal law any more.

But the roadmen, without any explanation, had begun to dig a new course for the stream. This seemed too much of a joke. A peasant, the son of Papasisto, ran back toward Fontamara, yelling at everyone on his way:

"Run! Do something about it! We'll have to tell the police and warn the mayor as soon as possible!"

There weren't any men in the village. In the month of June the men have too much to do in the fields. The women would have to go. But this was what happened with the women—you know how we are. The sun was already high and we hadn't started yet. Everybody was talking about it. All the women repeated what it was about, heard it repeated ten times from everyone who came by the door. But nobody started. I was at Elvira the dyer's, as I am every morning at that time. She had lost her mother a while back, and her father was helpless after the accident in the stone pit. I helped Elvira wash the old man. He grumbled and swore, and as usual was praying for death, to the great distress of his daughter. He didn't believe us when we told him about the roadmen. In short, nobody thought of going there. They simply couldn't tear themselves away from home. Some had children, others had chickens, pigs or goats, and still others had wash. Nobody could get going. We all had our own things to attend to. Then Marietta came forward because, she said, *she* knew how to deal with the authorities. She found another woman to go with her (I had better not tell you who), another woman who was also pregnant, though her husband had been in America ten years. It would be hard to believe that he did it from that distance.

"Should we let Fontamara be represented on an occasion like this by these women who are, after all, two whores?" asked Michele's wife in great agitation.

"You go, Matalè," said Elvira to me. "We have to make a good impression."

It would have been disgraceful and shameful for all of us if Marietta and the other one had represented the village. So we went to speak with Lisabetta Limona and Maria Grazia and talked them into coming to the city with us. Maria Grazia hid behind Ciammaruga, who hid behind Cannarozzo's daughter, who hid behind Filomena and Quaterna.

We had gathered in front of the church and were ready to go when Pilato's wife flew into a rage because we hadn't asked her to come along.

"You didn't want to let us know about it!" she shouted. "You want to feather your nest at our expense! Don't you think my husband's land needs water?"

We had to wait for her to get dressed. But instead of hurrying, she went to call Castagna, Recchiuta, Giuditta Scarpone and Fornara, and talked them

all into coming with us to town. Old Faustina
wanted to come too, the one whose husband had
been in prison for twenty years. But we said:

"What are you coming for? Your husband
doesn't need any water for his land."

"Suppose they let him out?" she asked us.

"You've been waiting for him for twenty years,
and he hasn't come out yet," we told her. "And
even if he did come out, who'd give him any money
to buy land?"

"Why don't you come out and say it? You'd be
ashamed if I came with you!" the old woman re-
torted. And she went back into her house so that
she wouldn't be seen crying.

There were about fifteen of us women all ready
to go. But we still had to wait in front of Baldissera's shop while Marietta curled her hair. Finally
she showed up in her Sunday clothes—the new
apron, a pearl necklace and that stupid little medal
with the portrait of the dead hero. So the sun was
high when we left the village. It was hot enough
to make you sick. Not even the dogs were out at
that time of day. Dust was all over, everywhere.

When the roadmen saw us going down toward
the plain, shouting and covered with dust, they got
scared and ran off through the vineyards.

Limona proposed that we go right back because
we'd done what we wanted to do. But Marietta,
with her new apron and her curled hair, said we
still had to go to the town because the roadmen

were acting on orders from there, not just for the fun of it. She knew how the authorities worked.

We were arguing what to do and deciding to go back when Marietta cut off all discussion:

"If you're scared," she said, "the two of us will go." And she got behind the other woman who was like her.

Therefore we all went off to town.

"We can't let Fontamara be represented on an occasion like this by these women who are, after all, two whores," we said. And we started again behind our leaders. The open road was like a furnace. The air was almost black. We went with our tongues out like a herd of sheep. I don't know where some of us found the energy to complain.

We stopped a moment to rest out of the sun beside the cemetery wall. Along the wall rose some of the tombs of the peasants who had got rich in America. They hadn't got rich enough to buy themselves a house and some land, but rich enough for a gentleman's tomb. We could hardly breathe in the shade.

We didn't get to town until about noon. The road dust had whitened us as if we had been at the mill, and a lot of the town people were scared when we showed up in the main square. We couldn't have looked very reassuring. The merchants came out of their shops and closed up in a great rush. Some fruit peddlers fled from the square with their baskets on their heads. The windows and balconies filled up with anxious faces. Some frightened clerks showed up on the steps of the town hall. Were they waiting for us to attack it? Actually, we did go up to the town hall in a compact group, but without any idea of what was going on in their minds. At that moment the constable shouted from a window of the town hall:

"Don't let them in! They'll fill the town hall with lice!"

With that the terror vanished as if by magic and everyone burst out laughing. The ones who were trembling with fright before, the ones who fled in terror, the ones who had closed up their shops, the ones who had run off with their baskets on their heads, all came back to make fun of us. We huddled up against the door of the town hall. Flattered with success, the constable began at the top of his voice to tell about Fontamara and its lice. There was a man holding his sides on a balcony opposite. The watchmaker, who had now reopened his shop, was crying with laughter. All the town clerks and some of the secretaries were on the steps, and they were howling.

In a calm voice I asked one of the women who stood near me:

"Aren't you ashamed?"

"Why?" she asked, laughing.

"Shame on anyone who laughs at the misery of others." I tried to explain it to her. "It's shameful to laugh at misfortune."

But she didn't understand me.

At any rate, we didn't know what to do. On the road Marietta had said she would handle it. But with all those people laughing she was confused. If it had been only the constable, she could have answered him back in kind, because he'd seen plenty of lice in his younger days, and not only on other people. But these were all city people. And we felt embarrassed because we were sweaty, dirty and dusty, and that's no way to come to the town hall.

One of the clerks took pity on us and asked:

"Whom are you looking for? Whom do you want?"

Marietta came forward and said:

"We came to speak to his honor the mayor."

The clerks on the threshold looked at one another, astounded. Some of them repeated the question.

"What do you want?"

"We want to speak to the mayor!" four or five of us answered. We were rapidly losing our tempers.

Then the clerks began laughing like madmen. They began repeating our request at the top of their lungs. "Guess what? They've come to talk with the mayor!" And laughter echoed from the square to the windows, from the windows to the balconies and from the balconies to the dining rooms of the nearby houses. Since it was noontime, the wives began calling their husbands home, warning them that the spaghetti was already on the stove. Some of the clerks left the town hall in a rush, and one of them closed the door. Before going away, the one who had been the least rude said:

"Do you really want to speak to the mayor? Wait for him here. You'll probably have to wait for him a long time."

It was quite a while before we found out what he meant. At the moment our attention was attracted by a fountain that we saw in a corner of the square. The sun and the dust had made our throats dry. Cabbages, potato peelings and other kitchen refuse were all floating in the basin of the fountain. It looked like one huge soup tureen. We had a fight about who was to drink first. We were all thirsty, but we couldn't all drink at once. Marietta's excuse that she was about to faint was recognized by no one. After much confusion some sort of order finally was set up. Several of us drank, and it became the turn of a girl who had sores on her lips. We wanted her to drink last, but she grabbed the edge of the fountain and wouldn't give up her place. Marietta was supposed to drink next, but suddenly there wasn't any more water.

It was probably a momentary interruption. We waited for the water to come back. But it didn't. The fountain had been silenced. We were about to go away, when we were attracted by the sound of the water. It had come back all of a sudden. There was another discussion. A couple of girls grabbed each other by the hair. Finally order was restored. But the water stopped again. There was no telling why the water acted like that. Nothing similar had ever happened at the fountain near the entrance to Fontamara. On the other side of the square the constable and the watchmaker observed us and laughed.

It may seem funny that I waste my time telling you about this, since worse things happened later. But I can't get over the way the water always got away from us. It was like this: when there wasn't any water we went away from the fountain, and when we were away the water came back. This happened three or four times. When we returned, the water dried up; when we left, the fountain started up again. We were dying of thirst and we couldn't drink. We could only look at the water from far away. If we went closer the water disappeared.

After the water had disappeared once more as we came up, about ten policemen approached, surrounded us and asked us in a nasty tone of voice what we wanted.

"We want to speak with the mayor," we answered.

And each one added her own complaint, because they were adding insult to injury with all these tricks.

"They're trying to steal our water!"

"We never saw such sacrilege! It's scandalous!"

"We'd rather give our blood than the water for our land!"

"If there's no justice, we'll make justice!"

"Where's the mayor?"

"The mayor!" yelled the local police chief. "Don't you know there aren't any more mayors? Now the mayor is called a *podestà!*"

It didn't matter to us at all what they called the man who ran the town. But it must have made a big difference to the educated people. Otherwise the clerks wouldn't have laughed so hard when we asked to speak with the mayor, and the police chief wouldn't have got so mad. Educated people are sticklers. They get mad about words.

The police chief told four policemen to take us to the podestà. Two policemen went in front of us and two in back. All the loafers watched this strange procession, shouting and making insulting gestures. The shopboys in town have always enjoyed making fun of the peasants. To our confusion, we realized that Marietta enjoyed a certain reputation among them. It was still worse when she began answering them back with the same bad words. Maria Grazia felt she was going to faint. Limona and I had to hold her up and help her to walk.

"O Jesus!" we said. "What sins have we committed more than the others that you punish us in this way?"

With the two policemen in front and back, we were like a captured herd.

"Matalè!" Limona said to me. "Let's go back home to Fontamara! What can we do here, Matalè? It's crazy!"

The policemen led us along the main street, then through several side streets. We got to the house of the former mayor, don Circostanza, but to our great surprise the policemen kept on going. We were truly surprised that don Circostanza wasn't the head of the town any more. We thought the policemen were taking us to don Carlo Magna's. But they went right on by without stopping. Soon we found ourselves outside the town among the meadows. Clouds of dust were rising from the burned street.

We said among ourselves: "The policemen are making fun of us. Nobody but don Circostanza could be the head of the town."

Groups of workers were eating their lunches in the shade of some pine trees, and others were resting with their heads on their folded-up jackets and their hats on their faces. The policemen didn't hide their bad humor. One of them barked at us:

"Why did you have to come right in the middle of lunch hour? Couldn't you come later?"

"Aren't we good Christians too?" we answered.

"You're peasants," he said. "You were made to suffer."

"What sins have we committed more than you? Don't you have mothers and sisters at home? Why do you talk like that? Just because we haven't fancy clothes?"

"It's not that. It's just that you're peasants and were made to suffer."

The path along which the policemen were leading

us was full of construction material—bricks, presses, bags of cement, sand, and ironwork—and it was hard for us to keep together. In this way we got to the gate of a new villa belonging to a Roman known throughout the countryside as the Trader. The villa was adorned with paper lamps of all colors and flags as for a fiesta. In the courtyard we saw some exhausted women sweeping and beating some rugs. The policemen stopped in front of the villa's gate. None of us could hold back her surprise.

"What! They've made this thief the head of the town! A foreigner!"

"Since yesterday," said a policeman. "The telegram came yesterday from Rome."

"Once you start up this kind of business you never know when it's going to stop," I said.

When the Trader came to our part of the country three years ago, nobody had known who he was or where he came from. He looked like an ordinary traveling salesman. He got a room in a transient hotel. He began by buying apples in May, when they're still on the trees and when the peasants need cash. Then he began buying onions, beans, lentils and tomatoes. He sent everything he bought to Rome. Later he began raising pigs. Then he started dealing in horses. In other words, he was mixed up in everything—hens, rabbits, bees, animal skins, road construction, land, brickwork and vegetables. He was seen at all the fairs and in all the local markets. His appearance caused a new kind of disturbance. In principle, the old-time landowners held him in contempt and refused to deal with him. But the Trader gained control of them one by one. There wasn't a single important deal he hadn't had something to do with. Where did he get all that money? The suspicious old-time landowners naïvely reported him to the police as a counterfeiter. But the bank notes didn't turn out to be false. It was found that the Trader was backed by a bank which gave him the money he needed.

At Fontamara we knew about this discovery and for quite a while we talked about it. Not even General Baldissera knew what it was all about. This was the first of a series of incomprehensible events. We knew, a bit from experience and a little more from what we had heard, that a bank is for keeping money or for sending it from America to Italy or for changing it into a foreign money. But what did the bank have to do with business? What could the bank care about raising pigs, building houses, selling furs or making bricks? A lot of strange things began with this.

To explain the man's rapid prosperity, about which everyone was talking, someone said:

"The Trader has discovered America right here. That's what it is."

"America," someone who had been there answered, "America is far away and doesn't look like this."

"America is everywhere," the Trader said to those who told him about the argument. "It's everywhere. All you have to do is know how to find it."

"But how is it that a foreigner has found something where we were born that we didn't notice before he came?"

"America is in working," the Trader said to that, as he wiped the sweat from his brow.

"You mean we don't work?" they asked him. "The ones who work most are the poorest."

All joking aside, there was no doubt that he had discovered America in our part of the country. He had a recipe to make gold from pine needles. Some thought he'd sold his soul to the Devil for wealth, and maybe they were right. Anyway, the Trader's prestige increased enormously after the accusation of counterfeiting. He was the agent of the bank. He had a huge banknote factory at his disposal. The old-time landowners began to tremble before him. In spite of all this, we couldn't understand how he had gotten the job of mayor (or podestà, which was all the same to us).

As soon as the women who were cleaning in the courtyard saw us, they ran to call Rosalia, the Trader's wife. She was furious. She was already old, and she dressed like a city woman. Her head was like a vulture's, balanced on top of a long, thin body.

"Get the hell out of here!" she began yelling at us in an insolent voice. "What do you want? Can't we even run our own house? Don't you know we're giving a party today? We have the nomination banquet in an hour! Nobody invited you! Go away! My husband's not home. And when he comes back he won't have time for you. If you want to talk to him, go find him at the brick factory!"

"We brought them here," said one of the policemen apologetically, "because they want to present a petition to the head of the town."

"We want justice!" yelled Marietta, coming forward. "Authority exists for justice."

This was what Marietta had learned when she knew all those important people in her capacity as Widow of the Dead Hero.

She also said, "God gave us the water!"

"My husband is at the brick factory," said the Trader's wife, her vanity flattered.

The policemen showed us the way to the brick factory and left us.

"We have to go to lunch," they told us. "Be careful."

After a long walk we got to the furnace. We found about twenty workers and some carters who were loading bricks. They stopped working and yelled at us stupidly.

"Where are you from? Are you on strike? What strike?"

We must have looked a fright.

"Where's your boss?" one of us asked. "He has to give us justice."

"Justice. Hah! Hah! How much is that per pound?"

"Listen!" said one of the older workers to us in a benevolent voice, "go back to Fontamara. There's no arguing with the Devil."

Anyway the Trader wasn't there. He had been there just before and had just left, as the workers told us. Maybe he'd gone to the electric saw, but probably he would have left there too. It would be better to go look for him at the tannery. But the tannery was a long way off.

We didn't know where to go, so we stayed in the middle of the street. It was suffocating. Dust was in our eyes, and nobody would have known us with our clothes and hair all dust, and our teeth, throats and chests all full of sand. We were fainting with thirst and hunger.

"It's all your fault, you damned bitch!" yelled Limona at Marietta.

This was the start of a really awful scene. Little groups of two or three formed and each began fighting with the rest. Ponzio's wife even fought me.

"You dragged me here!" she yelled. "I didn't want to come. I had housework to do. I haven't time to waste outside the house, and I don't like to parade around the streets of the city like this."

"Are you crazy?" I answered. "Maybe you've had a sunstroke."

Giuditta and Cannarozzo's daughter grabbed at each other's hair and ended up on the ground. Maria Grazia helped the Cannarozzo girl, but Recchiuta jumped on her and they all ended up on the ground in a heap of dust. Luckily the yells were worse than the blows that everyone was taking and giving. Marietta especially, caught between Michele's wife and Limona, was yelling as if they were cutting her throat. But she'd only had her hair mussed up and a new apron ruined. Some workers from the furnace broke it up but that didn't make us feel any better. The sun, our thirst and our fatigue, together with the humiliation, had reduced us all to tears.

"We shouldn't have followed that witch," said Limona, indicating Marietta. "The Trader hasn't anything to do with running off the water. What are we here for anyway?"

"He is the authority," yelled Marietta. "Only the authorities can decide."

"Let's go to don Carlo Magna's!" Zompa's wife suggested. "The stream's going to be sent to his land, so it must be his doing."

We resumed our *Via Crucis*, going from the Herod to the Pilate station, exhausted and degraded. Some of us were crying. Several of us were lamenting in high voices as in a litany: "Who could have done it?"

"We'll hear more of this at home," Limona said. "When our husbands hear what we've been doing all day, they'll whip our hides."

"Maybe we came here for fun?" I answered.

"We came here for our families, for the land."

"They'll beat the hell out of us," said Limona, and she cried.

Don Carlo Magna's old house had a gate as high and wide as a church door so that the wagons could pass through at harvest, and a vast entrance hall, paved in stone. Since we couldn't all go in, we left most of the group at the gate and three of us went on. The usual suspicious and arrogant maid opened the door for us. I went up to her.

"Could we speak with don Carlo for a minute?" I asked.

"Don Carlo?" she said. "Right now? Have you brought any gifts? Do you want to speak with his wife?"

Just then the mistress, donna Clorinda, came out. She recognized us at once.

"Carmè," she asked the maid, "who let these people in?"

"After you stole our water, what do you want next, wine too?" said Zompa's wife.

Donna Clorinda didn't understand, and she couldn't understand. She led us into the big kitchen. "Don Carlo is in the dining room, eating," she said.

All kinds of hams, sausages, skins full of lard, sour apples, onions, garlic and mushrooms were hanging from the kitchen ceiling. There was half a freshly killed lamb on the table, and the smell from the ovens was so good you could have cut it with a knife.

"What do you want?" said donna Clorinda in a hard tone of voice. "Did those vagabonds outside the gate come with you? What has happened?"

Donna Clorinda was wearing a black dress with a lot of lace on her chest and a pure-black hat on her head. When you looked her in the face and listened to her voice, you understood why she was called the crow around there. She really ran that house. She dealt with the tenants, paid for what had to be done and decided on what was to be bought and sold. Otherwise they would have had nothing. Don Carlo Magna was a famous good-time Charlie, lady-killer, gambler, drinker and glutton, as well as a timid and lazy man. He would have wasted the last penny's worth of land left him by his father, don Antonio, who, though he was a very rich man in his old age, had died pushing his plow. It is truly said that it takes only two generations from shirtsleeves to shirtsleeves.

Don Carlo had married late, and donna Clorinda had been able to salvage only some bits and pieces from the general wreckage. There remained little of the vast and numerous lands that his ancestors had assembled, buying up at rock-bottom prices the lands that were confiscated from the parishes and monasteries—lands that good Christians didn't dare buy. Once don Carlo Magna had owned almost all of Fontamara. Then the girls he liked best had been forced to go to his house and cater to his caprices. But now the lands that donna Clorinda had brought him in dowry were the largest part of all that was left, and she kept these in her own name. It was known that she kept her eyes closed to her husband's worst vice—which had sown dishonor and bad feeling among the peasant families—just so that she might run things. The unchanging answer the servant had been giving for so many years to all the people who came to see don Carlo Magna was an excuse for his wife to keep an eye on even her husband's most minute affairs.

"And now you want to take our water too?" I said to donna Clorinda. "Isn't it enough that you've made us poor? Do you want to send us out to beg?"

"The water belongs to God," Limona said. "You can't take water from the land it has always washed. It's a sacrilege. It's a sin against creation. You will have to answer for this before the Eternal Throne."

When we were through telling her about the water, donna Clorinda was so pale we thought she would faint. You could tell from the rigid lines of her thin face that she was fighting back tears of rage.

"That devil! That devil!" she was muttering under her breath.

But she wasn't talking about her husband.

"He must have sold his soul to the Devil," she told us. "No law holds him back. If he stays here another couple of years he will eat us alive, with our houses, land, trees and mountains. He'll tear us to pieces. He and his damned bank will send us all out to ask for alms. Then they'll appropriate even that."

Thus we learned, between laments and curses, that the famous lands of don Carlo Magna, toward which the brook at Fontamara was being directed, had been bought a week ago at a bargain price by the Trader. There was no doubt that after he had irrigated them he would resell them at a profit.

"That man has really discovered America in these parts," I couldn't help saying. "The peasants have to cross the ocean to find America. But that brigand has found it here."

"Isn't there any law for him?" asked Zompa's wife. "Aren't God's commandments any good for him?"

"For the Devil, God's commandments are no good," I said, crossing myself.

"Now they've made him podestà," continued donna Clorinda. "The new government is in the hands of a gang of bandits. They call themselves bankers and patriots, but they're bandits without any respect for the old-time landowner. Just think of it, since he got to be podestà, two typewriters have already disappeared from the town hall. Believe me, the doors and windows will be gone within a month. The streetcleaners are paid with town money, but since this morning some of them have been working in the Trader's brick factory. The roadmen, paid with public money, are digging ditches to drain the water onto the land he stole from my husband. The town clerk, Innocenzo La Legge, do you know him? He has become the servant of the Trader's wife. I met him this morning with a basket of vegetables on his back that bent him as low as a dog. And this is only the beginning. Believe me, this brigand will ruin us all."

We got only this impression from the outburst: now the old-time landowners would have to repent. I must confess that I found a morsel of honey in all this bitterness. As they say, if you eat the sheep whole, you vomit up wool.

"Those robbers have finally been robbed," we explained to the women we had left outside the gate.

"Do we have to look for the Trader again?" some of them yelled. "When will we get done with all this?"

"Since we've come this far we might as well continue," said Marietta. "After we've been through all this, should we come back empty-handed?"

Thus we found our way back to the road leading to the podestà's villa. My knees hurt from too much walking, like on Good Friday when you do the Stations of the Cross on your knees without getting up. My feet were on fire and my head was spinning.

On the road we met La Zappa, a goatherd from Fontamara, who was looking for the Trader too. He had been with his goats in the pasture when a game warden had warned him that he had to go away because that piece of pasture was going to be plowed for the Trader.

"Does the pasture belong to the Trader?" the goatherd had asked, laughing. "Then the air is his too!"

We knew La Zappa as a rather stupid boy, but this time he was right. Probably the guard had been having fun with him. The pastures had always been held in common. They were held in common from our mountain all the way to Puglia. In the month of May, after the Foggia fair, an interminable river of sheep would come each year to spend the summer, grazing until October in our mountains. They say it was like this before Christ was born. Many things have happened since then—wars, invasions, squabbles, quarrels between kings and popes—but the pastures have always been common property.

"Now the Trader has gone crazy," we said. "He thinks he can even take over a pasture. Or maybe he's not mad. Maybe the guard wanted to have fun with the people from Fontamara."

At the gate of the Trader's villa we found the maid completely desperate.

"The master hasn't come back yet!" she whimpered. "The men have been eating for half an hour and the guest of honor hasn't got here yet."

"We won't go away until we have had satisfaction," we said.

Some of us sat on the grassy edge of the path, and some on the piles of bricks.

The smell from the casseroles came out even to us. The maid began to tell us in great detail how the banquet had gone. There had been a toast by don Circostanza. Then she told us about the food, mostly in diminutives—little onions, small mushrooms, tiny potatoes, and so forth.

The banquet must have been nearly over, because they were already feeling the effect of the wine. Don Circostanza's strong voice dominated everybody else's. We could catch the echo of the discussion through the open windows. At a certain point a violent argument about the Omnipotent started up. The curate, don Abbacchio, and the druggist had the greatest possible difference of opinion. Don Circostanza's view was asked.

"The Omnipotent?" he yelled. "But it's perfectly clear that *omnipotent* is an adjective!"

Everybody burst out laughing. They agreed, and peace was made.

Then don Abbacchio's tipsy voice resounded forth in churchy tones:

"In the name of the fodder, and of the bun, and of the cold black toast, amen!"

An outburst of laughter greeted this witticism of the priest.

There was another pause. Then in his church voice don Abbacchio sang:

"*Ite, missá est!*"

That was the signal for the end of the banquet.

According to custom, the banqueters began to go into the garden to urinate.

Don Abbacchio came down first. He was fat and

puffed. The veins of his neck were swollen, his face was purple and his eyes were half closed in a beatified expression. The churchman could hardly stay on his feet for drunkenness. He made water against a tree in the garden, leaning his head against it so as not to fall.

Afterward the lawyer, the druggist, the tax collector, the postmaster, the notary and other men whom we didn't know came out, and they all made water against a pile of bricks.

Then came the lawyer, don Ciccone, with a young man who held him by the arm. He was blind drunk. We saw him kneeling in his own wet behind the brick pile. Meanwhile the maid, who had stayed on the lookout close to us, signaled the approach of the Trader.

I hurriedly crossed myself and held tight to the crown of my rosary, which I wore under my blouse. Meanwhile he approached, discoursing heatedly with some workers. He was in work clothes with his jacket on his arm, a water level in one hand, a large ruler sticking out of his pants pocket, his shoes white with lime, his pants and shoulders dirty with chalk. No one who didn't know him would think he was the richest man around and the new director of the town. Even when he knew we were there, the Trader kept on talking loudly with the workmen who were with him. He answered our greeting in a rush, touching his hat brim with two fingers.

"I haven't any time to waste!" he told us at once.

"We don't either," we answered him. "We're looking for justice and nothing else."

"You can talk to me about that at the town hall, not at home," he answered.

"You weren't at the town hall," I said, but my voice shook.

"I wasn't at the town hall because I haven't any time to waste," he answered angrily. "I like to work. I don't like to fiddle around!"

"Ah, you've discovered America right here," I told him, holding my rosary in one hand, "but don't think you're the first one who ever worked around here."

Marietta came up to explain our request, but the Trader didn't pay any attention to her and started bawling out the workers who were with him.

"If the carter keeps on breaking the tiles," he said, "I'll pay him with the pieces. What? He wants last month's pay? Shameless! Is he afraid that I'm going to abscond? Instead of thanking me for giving him work in time of crisis! Don't the cement workers want to work ten hours a day? Is that too much? But I work twelve hours a day. I'm the boss, but I work twelve hours a day."

"Ah, you've discovered America right here!" I yelled at him. "But you can't get away with it. . . . You mustn't think we're poor because we're lazy."

"Rosalia!" He called toward the villa, and his

wife appeared on the balcony. "Rosalia, has the architect brought the project? . . . Does that man think I'm paying him to eat? . . . Has the station-master brought the release? . . . He hasn't? I'll have that bastard transferred to Calabria! . . . Has the head guard come? . . . You sent him away? . . . Why did you send him away? . . . Banquet? What banquet? Ah, you mean the banquet for my nomination. . . . I'm sorry, I haven't the time. . . . I can't come. I absolutely have to find the head guard. . . . The guests will be offended? . . . Don't worry; they won't be offended. I know them well. Give 'em plenty to drink and they won't be offended. . . . Crap! I know them, I tell you."

The way he talked and acted told you a lot. We listened with our mouths open.

"If this fellow stays here two more years," I said to myself, "he'll certainly be running everything."

La Zappa ran after him and said to us:

"You women wait here!"

We saw him disappear behind a house under construction and we waited for him to return. We were bewildered, frightened and nearly hypnotized.

By this time the drunken banqueters had assembled on the balcony of the villa. Don Circostanza stood out among them like a sore thumb, with his melonlike head, his nose as porous as a sponge, his ears like fans and his belly at the third stage. It is known that the lawyers around our town have trousers called accordion trousers or richman's trousers especially made for banquets. Such trousers have three flies instead of one so that they can be gradually let out as the belly feels the need. That day all the gentlemen's trousers were at the third stage, and it wasn't hard to understand why.

As soon as don Circostanza recognized us, he came up to us with open arms.

"My beloved people of Fontamara!" he cried. "What has happened? What's all the fuss about?"

"Let everyone take care of his own affairs," I answered him. "But if it wouldn't disturb your digestion, we would like to bring you a petition."

Don Circostanza, who was also known as the People's Friend, had always—as he so constantly reminded us—had a special place in his heart for Fontamara; he was our protector, and it would require a long litany to do justice to him. He had always defended us, but he had ruined us as well. All the lawsuits of Fontamara came through his office, and most of Fontamara's hens and eggs had been ending up in his kitchen for the last forty years as payment to the People's Friend.

At one time when the franchise was restricted to those who could read and write, he sent a schoolteacher to Fontamara who taught all the peasants to write don Circostanza's name. From then on Fontamara voted unanimously for him. On the other hand, they could do nothing else even if they had wanted to, because they could write only that name. Then followed a period when the deaths in

Fontamara were reported to don Circostanza instead of to the town. He very artfully caused the dead to stay alive on paper, so that at each election they voted as he intended. The family of each of the living-dead received for consolation five lire each time. The Losurdos, who had seven living-deads, got thirty-five lire. We had two who were actually in the cemetery but alive on paper (our son, God rest his soul, dead at Tripoli, and the other at the stone pit), and at each election they too were faithful voters for don Circostanza, and for this we were paid ten lire each time. You can understand how the number of living-deads got to be pretty big as the years rolled by. The payment became a good source of income for the poor people of Fontamara. It was an income we didn't have to work very hard to earn, and it was the only time we were paid instead of paying.

This advantageous system was called—in the language of the People's Friend—*democracy*. And thanks to the sure and faithful support of our dead, don Circostanza's democracy always won. Though we had some serious disillusionments from don Circostanza, who often deceived us in collusion with don Carlo Magna, we never dared separate from him and look for another protector, chiefly because he held us through our dead people, who because of him were not completely dead and who were worth five lire apiece to us. This was no fortune, but better than nothing. As a result of this system, it came about that there lived at Fontamara a large group of men more than a hundred years old, a group very much out of proportion to the size of the village. For a while this constituted our claim to fame throughout the countryside. Some attributed long life to the waters around us, others to the air, and still others to the plainness of our food and even to our misery. According to don Circostanza, many rich men of the nearby villages who suffered from diseases of the liver and stomach or from gout openly envied us for all this good health and longevity. The number of the living-deads climbed to such a point that even when some of the peasants began voting against him in resentment of the support he gave to our greatest oppressor, don Carlo Magna, he was always assured a majority.

"The living betray me," don Circostanza bitterly remarked. "But the good souls of the dead are still faithful."

Then it happened, when nobody expected it, that he didn't want to pay us the usual consolation for the service that our dead rendered him. The pretext, to which we gave scant credit, was that the elections had been abolished. We didn't know what to think of this turn of events. We talked it over for months and months and never succeeded in resigning ourselves to the new circumstances. How could we admit that all our dear ones were suddenly so useless and that they must now all die permanently?

Every once in a while some widow or some mother

would go to don Circostanza to claim the five-lire consolation for the living-dead relative, but he wouldn't see her, and as soon as he heard the living-deads mentioned, he would fly into a rage and slam the door in her face. The people who still dared to insist on that antique right were getting rarer and rarer. Being right is no good, as General Baldissera said, unless you know how to defend yourself. And one day the same Baldissera came back to Fontamara very much excited, claiming that the time of the living-deads had returned. At least he thought so, because in the city he had seen a procession of men in black shirts lined up behind black banners. There was a skull and crossbones on the flags and on the men's shirts.

"Could they be our dead people?" Marietta had asked, as she thought of the ones she had lost and of the five-lire consolations. But the General hadn't recognized anyone from Fontamara.

"Hurrah for Fontamara!" don Circostanza shouted to us from the Trader's balcony.

The voice reassured us not a little. We didn't feel alone any more. We were so tired and discouraged that we could confuse that old rascal with an angel sent by God.

"The presence of these worthy ladies of Fontamara will make it possible for us to complete the telegram which we have decided to send to the head of the government," remarked don Circostanza to the gentlemen who were with him on the balcony.

He pulled a piece of paper out of his pocket, and after having added a few words, he read aloud:

" 'People and authorities together applaud the nomination of the new podestà.' "

When we realized that the guests had started to take leave of the lady Rosalia and were going to go away without hearing us, and that the Trader wasn't coming back, we lost our temper. We lined up across the gate, having decided to let no one go by before our case had been heard and before we had been assured that the brook would not be deviated. To this gesture we added the cry:

"Shame on you for treating the poor this way! Thieves! Thieves! We've been on the road all morning and nobody has heard us yet! We're Christians too! The wrath of God be upon you!"

Some of the most excited of us picked up some stones and threw them against a window of the second floor. Glass flew about. Excited by the sound of the broken glass, others threw themselves toward a pile of bricks behind the gate. The drunken men who were in the garden and who were about to go out got frightened and returned to the villa. The maid closed the French windows hurriedly. There was a moment of panic among the guests.

"It's the revolution!" cried the communal secretary. "Call the police!"

But at that moment we heard the Trader's voice behind us. It was strangely calm.

"What are you doing with my bricks?" he asked

us, laughing. "The bricks are mine and you can't take them even to stone me. Furthermore, there is no need to stone me. I am here to give you the explanations you want."

We put the bricks back on the piles and went into the garden at the Trader's invitation. We were on one side and the Trader with his frightened guests was on the other. The Trader's calm astounded us.

"Perhaps he isn't a man but a devil," whispered Maria Grazia to me, taking my arm. "Take a good look at him. Doesn't he look like a devil to you?"

"Maybe," I answered. "How else could he discover America around here? He is no better educated than don Circostanza and no more hard-working than our men."

"He must be a devil," said Maria Grazia, and she crossed herself quickly so nobody would notice.

Marietta came forward, put her hand on her heart where the medal was and with careful words spoke of the dirty trick of the roadmen who had turned our brook from its course.

"It's a sacrilege! I am sure you gentlemen will punish the roadmen for their crime," she concluded.

"If a crime has been committed," said the Trader, "you may be assured that I will know what to do about it. There will be no crimes as long as I am head of the town. But I am afraid you have been misinformed. There is no crime here. Secretary, explain what has happened."

From the guests the secretary came forth, timid and evidently still drunk. Before he began talking he took off his straw hat.

"There is no crime!" stammered the secretary. "Honest. Under the new government there can be no crimes. Crimes? Never! It's a forbidden word. It's all perfectly legal. As a matter of fact, it's a favor the authorities have decided to confer on Fontamara."

When he said "favor" he looked at everybody with a smile. Then he took some paper out of his pocket and began talking faster:

"Here is a petition with the names of the peasants of Fontamara. That is, of all your husbands with no exceptions. The petition asks the government 'in the interests of superior production' to change the course of the stream from the insufficiently cultivated lands of Fontamara to the lands of the town, 'whose proprietors can invest more capital.' I don't know if you women can understand these things."

The secretary wanted to add something, but we interrupted him. We knew that a certain Cavaliere Pelino had written the names of all the peasants of Fontamara on the blank sheets of paper.

"Cheaters! Fakes! Thieves!" we protested. "You study law to deceive the poor! That's a false petition!"

The Trader tried to say something, but we wouldn't let him. Our patience was exhausted.

"We don't want any more hot air," we shouted. "Enough speechifying! Every time you open your mouth you tell a lie. The water is ours and will always be ours. By Christ, we'll burn your villa!"

The words expressed our state of mind exactly. But don Circostanza re-established calm.

"These women are right!" he shouted, leaving his colleagues and coming to us. "They are right— ten, a hundred and a thousand times right!"

At this point we became faithful and silent once more. Don Circostanza had undertaken our defense and we knew he was a great lawyer. For some reason the sound of his voice made us feel like little girls. Some of us couldn't hold back our tears.

"These women are right," the People's Friend went on. "I have always defended them and will continue to do so. Basically, what is it that these women want? They want to be respected——"

"That's right!" interrupted Marietta, and she ran up to kiss his hands.

"They wish to be respected and we must respect them," continued don Circostanza, extending a threatening arm towards the prominent citizens. "They deserve our respect. These women are not criminals. They know all too well that the law is against them, yet they do not want to go against the law. They want to do right by the podestà. They

have appealed to his heart. They have not appealed
to the head of the town, but to the benefactor, to
the philanthropist, to the man who in our poor countryside has discovered America. Isn't it possible to
get together?"

When don Circostanza had finished talking for
us, we thanked him and some of us kissed his hands.
He strutted about, pleased at our compliments.
Then there were various compromise proposals.
Don Abbacchio made various offers, the notary
made another and the tax collector made still another. But they were impossible because they didn't
take into account the scarcity of the water or the
methods of irrigation.

The Trader said nothing. He let the other people
talk and smiled with his extinguished cigar in a
corner of his mouth.

Don Circostanza presented the solution.

"These women claim that half the stream isn't
enough to irrigate the land. They want more than
half, as I interpret their needs. Therefore there is
only one possible solution. We must give three
quarters of the water to the podestà and the other
three quarters to Fontamara. Thus both will have
three quarters, a little more than half. I am sure that
my proposal will be very detrimental to the
podestà, but I appeal to his sentiments as a philanthropist and public benefactor."

The guests had now recovered from their fear
and had gathered around the Trader to beg him to

sacrifice in our favor. After having been pleaded with, the Trader finally gave in.

A piece of paper was brought out at once. I saw the danger right away.

"If there's something to pay, I'm not paying," I hastened to say.

"There is nothing to pay," said the Trader.

"Nothing?" said Zompa, her voice soft. "If there's nothing to pay, it's a swindle."

"If you really want to pay," I pointed out to her, "you certainly can."

"Not even if they wanted to blind me," she answered. "If it doesn't cost anything, it's a swindle."

"Then it would be better if you would pay," I said.

"Not even if they blind me," she repeated.

The notary scribbled the compromise on the paper and had it signed by the Trader, by the town secretary and by don Circostanza, acting in his capacity of representative of Fontamara.

After that we took the road home.

(Actually none of us understood what the compromise was all about.)

"At least it was free," repeated Marietta as in a litany. "At least it was free."

If you like, my husband can tell you what happened next.

3.

During the next few days the roadmen, under the protection of two armed guards, took up their work on the ditch that was to lead some of our water onto the Trader's land. But the question remained: exactly how much of the water was to be diverted?

"Mind your own business," every woman in Fontamara was saying to her man. "Don't get involved with the guards. Don't ruin your family. Let the others get into trouble."

Everyone waited for someone else to get in trouble. Passing by the armed guards on the way to work in the morning or coming back in the evening, everyone tried to look the other way. In this way nobody committed himself. But we were pretty angry, and we couldn't talk about anything else.

"When bad luck starts, who can stop it?" we said among ourselves. "Maybe the worst is still to come."

Our lack of education prevented us from understanding how the water could be divided into two equal parts each containing three quarters. The very women who had accepted the compromise for us did not agree as to what it really meant. Some claimed that the water was to be divided into two equal parts, others that Fontamara was to get more than half, that is, three quarters. Michele Zompa finally came to the conclusion that the three quarters referred to the moon in the sense that the brook was to irrigate the land in Fontamara during three phases of the moon, and the Trader's land in the following three phases, and so on.

Nobody knew enough to see through the swindle, because we had been taught to do little more than write our own names. We were afraid to go to some literate person for fear of adding expenses to the swindle. Thus, every evening as we sat on our thresholds, eating soup from a plate held on our knees, there was nothing so actively discussed as the swindle. There were many suppositions and endless and useless chatter, always the same chatter. There was very definitely a swindle, but what kind of swindle? One evening General Baldissera broke out into one of his usual unbridled and extravagant invectives against injustice that injures the innocent but is avenged by the infallible hand of the Law.

"I'll go there myself," he yelled in an indignant and choleric voice. "I'll go there and tell those people what the Law is and what the Law was and what the Law will always be."

But his ardor never produced any results, not only because of his old age but also because of his timidity. When he was a little boy at Fossa and worked as a shoemaker, he learned etiquette from an old baron who had fallen on hard times and for whom on Sunday afternoons he performed the ancient and dignified office of *domenichino*. The job was unpaid but satisfying and not at all tiring, since it consisted only in walking along at a respectful distance behind his honor the baron on his Sunday stroll. The baron was in greatly reduced circumstances, often not having enough money to eat, let alone pay a servant. He lived in a corner of the decayed family mansion, from which the creditors had taken away all the furniture and everything else that could be moved, leaving him only a bed with a canopy and an easy chair. He lived ignored and despised by the rest of the world—but he was never able to give up his Sunday stroll. Nor could he disgrace the family name by taking the walk alone. All this had been many years before, but Baldissera still remembered everything about this fallen nobleman, much of which he had to invent. This was the amusing part of it. We let him talk because we saw that it did him good.

General Baldissera was very poor, perhaps the most impoverished man in Fontamara, but he didn't want anyone to know about it, and he resorted to all sorts of tricks to conceal the hunger that had been devouring him for many years. Among other things, he would go away on Sunday under the strangest of pretexts and come back in the evening, actually as sober and hungry as ever, but weaving slightly and holding a toothpick in his mouth to give the impression that he had eaten meat and had drunk too much—as if he could afford his caprices.

In this state of feigned drunkenness, he liked to tell us all the details of heated discussions and encounters with important people in the town, mostly creditors of the late baron.

"Ah, if you had seen me, if you had heard me!" he would say with a self-satisfied expression on his face.

There were two or three of us, his old friends, who knew that it was all made up, but in order not to rob this miserable man of that one pleasure we said nothing.

The dispute about the water caused us to be honored with a visit from don Abbacchio. One evening, panting and sweating, he came to Fontamara in a surrey behind a fine horse and sent for some of us older people because he had something important to tell us.

"You see what sacrifices I make for you," he said to us. "I have come here because I like you more than myself. For the love of God, don't get involved with the Trader!" he warned us in the gloomy voice he used to preach to us about hell. "He's a terrible man, a demon the like of which has never been seen around here. Be patient. It's better for you. All you can do is pray to God."

"If he's a demon, why don't you exorcise him?" asked old Zompa.

Don Abbacchio responded with a gesture of resignation. "Maybe he's not a demon but a devil. The Church can't do anything about it. You are too ignorant to do anything about it. You are too ignorant to understand these things."

"A real devil?" I asked.

"For all I know, he's Satan himself," answered the priest.

"Why doesn't he have horns and goat's feet?" I asked him.

"It isn't that way any more. Satan's very smart."

The priest's words made a strong impression on us, especially when Baldovino told us that he had found out from the coachman that the surrey don Abbacchio had used to come to Fontamara belonged to the Trader. Truly, a demon with the priests on his side had never been heard of before. And we were too ignorant to understand it. Therefore each one of us looked to his own welfare at the expense of the others instead of trying to fight the demon. Each tried to get the best of what little water was left. It was still several weeks before irrigation time, but the arguments and discussions began right away.

In those days most of us went to Fucino to get jobs helping with the harvest. We had to get up before dawn to be at Fucino before the sun rose and wait there for someone to call us. Our mortification was beyond words. At one time only the poorest of peasants had been forced to offer themselves on the square in that manner, but now the times were hard for all of us. What little acreage we small landowners had was all tied up in mortgages and produced barely enough to pay the interest on our debts, so we had to work as day laborers to keep alive. The large landowners and overseers soon took advantage of the great number of laborers and lowered the pay. But low as this was, there were always peasants so hungry that they had to accept it. Some of them were at the point of offering themselves without the pay being decided on beforehand, so ready were they to accept any kind of miserable amount. From the marketplace in Fossa to Fucino, accordingly as the strips of land were placed, we had to go from six to nine miles, which were in addition to the three miles to the marketplace. And we had to go all that way back home. Every evening I felt as exhausted and degraded as a beast.

"I'm not getting up tomorrow. I can't stand on my feet. Just let me die in peace!" I said to my wife.

But at three in the morning, as soon as the rooster crowed, I would wake my son, and we would drink a glass of wine before taking the road to work.

As the peasants of Fontamara went to and from work, the fights over the water got steadily more violent. Between myself and my brother-in-law, Pilato, things threatened to come to blows, because neither of us was disposed to sacrifice himself for the other. We both went to work along the same road with our sons, but we didn't speak. We kept looking at each other as if a fight were brewing.

One morning when I was coming down to Fossa

with my son, I met Pilato as he was talking with the roadmen.

"Look," he said, "all I care about is that you leave some water to my beans. Let the rest die off!"

Whom could he have been talking about except me?

"You'll die off first yourself!" I yelled, coming at him with a pruning hook.

Berardo Viola and the two guards came up, so the fight was avoided for that day. As a matter of fact, Berardo went with us to Fucino for several days to prevent a repetition. He could be indifferent as far as the water was concerned for the simple reason that he had no land, either with or without water, and he thus had no interests in conflict with the other peasants.

The land he had inherited from his father had been sold to don Circostanza to pay for a lawsuit and to buy passage to America. At that time Berardo was thinking of emigrating and, once he had made his fortune, never returning to Fontamara. All this was the result of his having been extremely upset when a man from Fossa whom he had known in the army had, as he put it, betrayed him. He had formed a great friendship with this man and had shared his last crust with him on several occasions. In a fight near Fossa, Berardo had once cracked several heads to defend this friend, and he had come back to Fontamara satisfied that he had been of service to him and had not been recognized by anyone else. This same friend, however, saved his own skin by reporting Berardo to the police. Berardo was deeply offended and for several days didn't know what to do to get even with the false friend. Because he really liked this man from Fossa, he decided merely not to see him again and to go far away from our village. Our advice and the pleadings of his mother were both useless.

"If you already have land, why do you want to go to America?" we asked him.

"I won't stay here," he answered. "This place stinks."

The only one who encouraged him to go was don Circostanza. "If you stay here, you'll die in prison," he kept telling him.

So Berardo sold his land to don Circostanza, and with some of the money he bribed the people he had beaten up in Fossa to keep silent, and with the rest he bought his ticket. But before he left there came a new law, about which don Circostanza had perhaps previously been informed, suspending all emigration. And so Berardo had to stay at Fontamara, like an unleashed dog that doesn't know what to do with its freedom and desperately circles around the good thing it has lost.

Nobody thought he was wrong. How can a man of the soil resign himself to the loss of his land? The land had belonged to Berardo's father, and Berardo had worked on it since he was ten years old. Where we live, and probably in other places as well, the relationship between the farmer and his land is a long, hard business, not unlike marriage. It's a sort of sacrament. Just buying land doesn't really make it yours. It gets to be yours after long years of sweat, tears and exhaustion. If you have land you don't sleep nights when the weather is bad; even if you're dead tired, you can't sleep, for you don't know what's happening to it. In the morning you run to see how it is. If someone else takes your land, even if he gives you money for it, it's always a little as if he had taken your wife. Even when land is sold, it carries for a long time the name of the man who first had it.

Everyone knew what was wrong with Berardo. And Maria Rosa, his mother, seeing her son suffer for his useless sacrifice of the land and knowing that he was a violent and impulsive man, asked me one day to take her to don Circostanza's. She had a cockerel and a dozen eggs to give him, and when she went up to him she kissed his hands, kneeling in front of him. She begged him to give back her son's land on the condition that Berardo give him part of the produce for a few years. It didn't do any good. The lawyer explained that he had not bought the land to cultivate it but to get the lime underneath. (In fact, there is now a deep, wide crater on the land in which several workers use their picks and little carts.) He threatened to call the police if she didn't go away, but added:

"If Berardo would like, I could take him on as a workman in the pit."

This was adding insult to injury, and we didn't even mention this to Berardo.

This cave, this ever-widening and deepening ditch, became like a hole in Berardo's heart. "Pretty soon," we were saying to ourselves, "he'll do something awful. He'll come to a bad end like his grandfather." And poor Maria Rosa had a novena for his salvation secretly said at San Giuseppe da Copertino, and sold two sheets to light some candles before the saint so that her son might be saved.

But one day, as we found out later, Berardo went to the lawyer's office himself. Having pushed aside the maid, who had tried to tell him that don Circostanza was out, he looked for him in all the rooms and found him hiding behind some window curtains.

"Squire," he said with great calm (as he later put it, with respect), "you have assured me several times that I would die in prison; don't you think it's time that I went there?"

The lawyer must have understood that his life was hanging by a thread, but he managed to smile.

"Why are you in such a hurry?" he stammered.

"This would be just the time," explained Berardo, who *was* in a hurry. "This is the only time I could go with a clear conscience!"

"You always think of farming," said the lawyer.

"Why haven't you tried some other occupation?"

"Why don't trout fly? And why don't sparrows swim?" answered Berardo. Then he added threateningly, "I'm a peasant and I need land."

"There's some other land—of a different type," answered don Circostanza. "I'm surprised you haven't thought of it yourself. Sit down and listen to me. Above Fontamara, around Serpari, in the valley between the rocks, there's a little meadow that belongs to the town and is used only by an occasional goat but nothing else. It's good land, and if you want to work it, I can have the town sell it to you at a good price."

That's how don Circostanza saved himself. Berardo got his bit of land near Serpari at a good price and was landless no longer. But he had to work like a dog to get it ready, from night to morning and on holidays, because he had to hire out during the day like the other peasants. When we started the donkey off at dawn, we saw Berardo coming down the mountain with his hoe on his shoulder, and when we went back into the house after having eaten our soup, we saw Berardo going up the mountain.

"You'll kill yourself that way," we said to him. "You shouldn't ruin yourself."

"Either the mountain's going to kill me, or I'm going to kill the mountain!" he answered laughing.

"Don't talk like that!" Michele Zompa warned

him. "You can act as you please, but you mustn't tempt fate."

But we all really liked Berardo. He had his defects, especially when he was drunk, but he was loyal and sincere and had had a lot of hard luck, so we really hoped that he could win back the land. But the day he told us he had planted a bag of maize in the Serpari area (where nobody had ever heard of anything being planted before), we all shared his joy and drank his health.

"I've broken in the old mountain," said Berardo, laughing.

Maybe we were too happy, or maybe we had tempted fate, just as Michele had feared.

We all know what happened two months later. Although the old people used to tell of similar things, this was something we won't easily forget, because everyone believes what he sees with his own eyes. Some things should be told in a few words, for thinking about them doesn't do any good. At any rate, it rained steadily for three days, but not in an exceptional quantity. The top of the mountain over Fontamara was wrapped in a black cloud that concealed everything. And on the dawn of the third day a torrent of water came down from the mountain in the direction of Serpari as if the mountain were collapsing, and this torrent took away Berardo's little field as fast as a starving man gobbles up a plate of soup, digging up the soil down to the rocks and scattering the little maize seedlings all over the valley. There was a great ditch where the field had been—a deep, wide crater.

The ones who don't know about this or who have forgotten are unfair to Berardo and prefer to explain his destiny in terms of his grandfather, the famous bandit Viola—the last bandit around here—whom the Piedmontese executed. It is certain, however, that Berardo had fought hard luck all his life, and he never seemed to let any bad break keep him down for long.

But how can you fight your luck? The worst was the following (and it's a detail that oughtn't to be forgotten): when we saw the torrent coming down the mountain, everyone was terrified but nobody seemed particularly surprised, Berardo least of all. We were all in the square in front of the church and he was with us.

"I knew it all the time," he said, and he never said anything else. His mother stood clinging to his shoulder, petrified with terror, with a face like a corpse's or like Mary's at Calvary. And he kept on saying:

"I knew it all the time. I just knew it!"

According to the old people who remembered his grandfather, Berardo had inherited his physical characteristics from him. He was very tall and as sturdy as an oak trunk; his neck was short and bull-like and his head square, but he had very gentle eyes. He still had the eyes of a little boy when he was a man. It was incomprehensible and even ridiculous that a man as strong as that could have the eyes and smile of a child.

His perdition and his ruin, as I have already said, were his friends; he would have given the shirt off his back to a friend. "If he's really going to end up like his grandfather," his mother used to say, "it won't be for money but for friends."

Because of his physical superiority he had a prestige among the boys in Fontamara that easily put their fathers in second place. It would take too long to tell you all of Berardo's exploits. Let one suffice, the stupidest of them all. One night he put a donkey on his back and took it all the way up to the top of the church tower. But he often used his strength for less amusing things. Whenever we heard of anything violent, if it was Berardo's doing, we knew it right away. He never let the people from the city get away with anything. To get back at them for the joke about the priest, he broke several places in the ditches that lead the water to Fossa. Another time the milestones on the national highway, which were built with cement, were entirely destroyed for a radius of ten miles. As for the signs showing the directions and distances to the people in cars, none of them stayed long in their places. And so when the lights went off for the first time in Fontamara, Berardo said not a word. But two evenings later the street lamps between the town and the nearby villages were all broken.

"There's no sense talking with the authorities." This was Berardo Viola's bitter doctrine. He explained:

"The law is made by townsmen, is applied by judges who are all townsmen, and is interpreted by lawyers who are all townsmen. How can a farmer ever be right?"

If anyone made the objection:

"But if the landlords lower farm hands' wages, is it bad to discuss that?"

His answer was glib:

"They'd just be wasting their time. The farm hands who argue with the landlords are just wasting their time. The pay would still be less. A landlord is never moved by arguments. The landlord acts according to interest. He won't cut your pay if it is against his best interest. And how could that be? Very simple. The boys' pay for the weeding was cut from seven to five lire. Following my advice, they did not protest. But instead of uprooting the weeds, they simply covered them with earth. After the rains in April the landlords realized that the weeds were higher than the plants. What little they would have gained by cutting wages they lost ten times over at harvest time. The pay of the harvesters goes down? It's useless to talk about it. There is more than one way of harvesting grain. There are ten ways, and each way corresponds to a certain rate of pay. If the rate of pay is good, the work will be good. If the rate of pay is bad, the work will be bad."

If someone asked him:

"Now that the Trader wants to steal our water, shouldn't we talk about that?"

His answer was just as simple:

"Set fire to the tannery and he'll give you back your water without discussion. And if he still doesn't understand, set fire to his wood. And if that isn't enough, blow up his brick furnace. And if he is still so stupid he doesn't understand, burn his villa some night when he's in bed with donna Rosalia. That's the only way you can get your water back. And if you don't, one day the Trader will take away your daughters and sell them on the market. And that would be a good idea, but what are your girls worth?"

This was the bitter view of Berardo Viola.

But he thought that way because he had lost his land. And this must have hurt him very much. He thought the way people think when they have nothing to lose. The others were better off. After he had lost his land and had worked at all kinds of things in their various seasons—as a day laborer, as a forester, as a coal heaver and as a bricklayer— he had descended below the farmers and had no right to think that they would follow his lead. Hence there was always great confusion when he entered our discussions. No older man would listen to him or even contradict him, except General Baldissera, who held principles entirely in opposition to Berardo's, but was by nature inclined to useless chatter. Yet with his extravagant speeches and even more by his example, Berardo had changed the opinions of all the young people in Fontamara.

We had never seen such lazy young people before. At one period they went off to look for work as soon as they were sixteen years old. Some of them went to Latium, some to Puglia, and the most eager of them to America. Many of them left their fiancées for four, six and even ten years; the girl swore to be faithful and she married him when he got back. Others got married the day before the boy left, and after the first night of love they were separated for four, six and even ten years. And when they got back, they found their children already grown up—and sometimes they found several of various ages. But the ban on emigration had interrupted the departure of the young people. They were obliged to remain at Fontamara, so that there was less work for everyone. The anti-emigration law meant that it was impossible to save the little nest egg that would rescue the ancestral land from the debts and mortgages, that would permit some improvements, that would permit the substitution of a new donkey for the old or dead one, that would make possible buying a pig, two goats, or a bed in which to put a wife. Because they were young they found no relief in lamenting or complaining, nor did they seem to be aware of how hard their lot was. But on the many days when they had nothing to do they were all together, and under the influence of the one who was oldest and stupidest were prone to do things and think up enterprises that were very unwise.

In the winter they usually gathered in Antonio La Zappa's stall, where the goats' breath made the air warmer. Spaventa's son and Della Croce, Palummo, Raffaele Scarpone and Venerdì Santo went there with my son and Pilato's and other young men. Berardo would show up whenever there was something to be organized. No one else was admitted to the company, which the girls used to call the Vice Club. And the name of Vice Club was more suitable than we first thought, because, as we found out later, there were relations between those boys and the goats, and this traffic went on for a long time. As always in such cases, the last people to hear about it were the people who owned the goats. But later the ones who entrusted the beasts to La Zappa took them back and the Vice Club was dissolved. The boys met elsewhere, behind the church or among the ruins of don Carlo Magna's old palace or in Marietta's place, waiting for Berardo. If he didn't show up, the day was wasted; his presence created life. They chattered and played, but it was a way of killing time while waiting for him to come. If he invited them, they went with him, following behind, hanging on his every word with their mouths open.

But what was most surprising to us older men was to see a young man like Berardo (who was already almost thirty years old) be obliged to run errands for his mother, who was no longer young, and show no inclination whatsoever to get married.

"No woman could handle him," his mother kept saying. "I know him. I bore him. He's no lady's man."

"But he can't stay like that all the time," I answered. "A man needs a woman. You should talk to him about it."

"It's not God's will," said his sad and resigned mother. "This is perfectly clear by now. And besides, can you tell who sent all that water down from the mountain?"

"This wasn't the first flood," I answered. "And it won't be the last."

"God wants him a bandit," concluded his mother. "It's the fate of the Violas. This is obvious."

That's how old Maria Rosa spoke. She spent most of the day, and during the summer, the night, too, on a stone in front of the entrance to her house, which was really a cave, with only one true wall. In front of the cave Maria Rosa spun and cooked, waiting for the return of her son, whom she admired and boasted about in words mothers rarely use.

Since Berardo couldn't excel in riches, Maria Rosa found it entirely inevitable and appropriate that he excel in misfortune.

"The Violas are not home-loving men," said Maria Rosa with sadness and pride. "They aren't made to sleep between sheets. They aren't men for just one woman. In the nine months I carried him, my womb was black and blue from his kicks."

The whole affair would have been none of my business if it hadn't been for Elvira, who was the daughter of my sister Nazzarena—God rest her soul—who had died the year before. She was considered Berardo's intended in the village, even though they probably had never even spoken to each other. But when she went to church or to the fountain, Berardo got pale, held his breath and followed her with his eyes in such a way as to leave no doubt about his intentions.

And inasmuch as Elvira had found out immediately from her friends how Berardo felt, and had not protested or changed the time or place of her walks, it meant that she didn't disapprove. There had been nothing else between them, but Fontamara considered it quite natural that they should be engaged, since Berardo was the strongest man around and Elvira was the prettiest girl. Maybe there are prettier ones in the city, but we had never seen anyone so beautiful at Fontamara. More than beautiful, she was gentle and delicate, of medium size, with a sweet and quiet voice. Nobody had ever heard her laughing loudly, or giggling, or forgetting herself in public, or even crying. She was of an extraordinary reserve and modesty, like a little Madonna. When she was around, nobody dared to swear or say bad things. One day Palummo's son, who forgot this, was barely saved from Berardo's wrath. Elvira's friend told her about it right away, and on the next day she, who had never spoken to a young man on the street, apologized for this boy to Berardo when she met him. "It was my fault," she said.

Beyond all this, we knew that the girl had a sizable dowry: a thousand in cash and her hope chest all ready with sheets, pillowcases, towels, blankets of all kinds, a new cupboard, two walnut chests and a bedstead with two brass pieces—all paid for. Why was Berardo waiting?

One day I had a heart-to-heart talk with him. (This was after the flood.) I told him all this.

"What makes you think I can marry a girl with a dowry when I haven't any land?" he said, with tears in his eyes.

He was so strong and insistent that I didn't dare say anything more. If you asked him about Elvira, you were sure to make him furious. During the winter evenings when the old men drink and the young ones talk with their wives and girl friends, Berardo would argue deep into the night with General Baldissera about the difference between the city people and farmers, and about the three laws: the law of the priests, the law of the landowners and the law fixed by customs. He would pound the table until Marietta's little wineshop trembled. But this had no effect on General Baldissera, who was a believer in the "unchangeable order."

Because of this, you might think that Berardo wasn't interested in Elvira any more. But one day word got around that Filippo il Bello, the roadman, had proposed to her. Berardo really saw red. He dashed over to Filippo's house, but he wasn't home. When Berardo heard that he was at the gravel pit, he ran there as fast as he could and found him measuring some heaps of gravel. Without even asking him if it was true that he had proposed to Elvira, he picked him up and threw him onto the gravel several times before some of the other workmen came up.

From that time on, no one else showed any interest in Elvira. But Berardo continued to avoid her.

One day my wife was lamenting about this with Maria Rosa. And suddenly the old woman decided. "Let's go and see," she said.

I helped Maria Rosa close up the cave and we took a short cut to Elvira's house. It was a stony, narrow path that had been deeply cut by an old flood. The room we came into was paved in stone and it was so dark that you could barely see the stove in one

corner and in the other the low bed where Damiano
lay. He was paralyzed.

"Damià!" yelled Maria Rosa, looking at him
with obvious disgust. "Who put the evil eye on
you?"

As we arrived, Elvira had gotten up to light an
oil lamp, and then other faces came up out of the
darkness. It is our custom for those who have
nothing to do to visit the sick, sometimes for days
on end. In the dark corners of the room some women
were nursing their babies, some were making stock-
ings and others were telling stories of various
trials and tribulations. In the meantime Elvira
had gone back to her place by the bed, near her
father. She was wiping the sweat off his face with
a long napkin. The sweat was continuous and in-
exhaustible, like a fountain or a river.

"Damià," repeated Maria Rosa, looking suspi-
ciously at the other visitors, "who has put the evil
eye on you?"

From out of the darkness a woman spoke. She told
of a dream Nazzarena—God rest her soul—had
had when she bore Elvira. "I am giving you the
most beautiful of all my doves," the Madonna had
said to her. "But you and your husband will have
to pay for it with sore trials."

Then I called Elvira and we sat down on the
threshold with Maria Rosa. This was probably the
first time that Maria Rosa could see her up close
and notice what a fine girl she was. I saw the old

woman's eyes slowly light up as if she had found
something delightful, then dampen suddenly with
emotion.

"Daughter, I don't know if you know about the
Violas," she said, taking one of Elvira's hands in
hers. "They have a family curse nobody has ever
been able to explain to me. Berardo's grandfather
was hanged."

The girl grew pale at this and her tender hand
shook between the rough wooden ones of the older
woman.

"That's no reason to be ashamed, it seems to
me," she murmured.

"His father died in Brazil," continued the old
woman, "and nobody knows how he died. He used
to send me something every month to put away so
we could buy some land. Finally I was able to buy
land, but after that he never wrote again. Then
came the news that he had died, and we still don't
know how it happened."

"That's no reason to be ashamed," said Elvira.

"Berardo has no land," Maria Rosa added. "He's
very strong, not strong like a man but like a bull.
There was never a man as strong as he in Fontamara. He's strong enough to carry a donkey all
the way up to the top of the church tower, but he
can't beat the family curse."

"Does our luck seem any better?" asked Elvira,
pointing to her sick father.

"You love him that much?" shouted Maria Rosa, almost scandalized.

Elvira blushed and her answer was quicker than I had thought it would be:

"With your permission, I'll answer that question only if your son asks it."

But she spoke so humbly and so movingly that Maria Rosa had nothing more to say.

"She's an extraordinary girl," I said to the old woman as I took her back home, "and she has a good dowry. She could be the making of Berardo."

"More likely his ruin," said his mother angrily.

I didn't pay any attention to what she said, because Maria Rosa naturally sees things at their worst. But I told everything to my husband.

I never like to get involved in other people's affairs, but Damiano's illness forced me to keep an eye on Elvira, who was, as I have said, my sister Nazzarena's only daughter. Therefore one night coming back from Fucino with Berardo I tried to get him to talk.

"Elvira is nearly twenty-five years old," I said, "and for our village that's old. What's more, her father is ill. He can't help her to weave. Above all, Elvira needs a husband to protect her."

Berardo had stopped breathing.

"If you don't marry her," I told him, "she could marry someone else."

Suddenly, Berardo got mad.

"Stop it!" he said in a tone that allowed for no answer.

The next morning I waited for him in the square to go to Fucino, but he wasn't there. I went to his house to find out if he was angry with me, and I found his old mother in tears.

"Berardo's gone crazy," she told me. "He'll end up like his grandfather. Last night he didn't sleep a wink. He got up about two o'clock. I told him it was early to go to Fucino. I asked him where he was going and he told me to Cammarese. I asked him why he was going to Cammarese if there was work at Fucino, and he said because the pay was better. I asked him when he ever bothered about the pay. But he took a piece of bread and an onion and left without saying anything else."

Word got around that Berardo had left for the Roman country and everyone was surprised, though a peasant who lives by day labor has no obligation to stay in his village, even when there's lots of work to do, if he can get better pay somewhere else. But we were even more surprised when Berardo came back the same night.

There were four or five of us in the middle of the street. There were Marietta, Baldissera and old Zompa, and we were just talking about Berardo. He must have gotten it into his head to win his land back as soon as possible, we were saying. But how can he do it, we said, if he can barely keep alive on his day labor?

"He'll work twice as hard," said Marietta. "He'll find some work for the nighttime."

"It'll ruin his health," I said. "He'll get his land all right, but in a cemetery." But nobody suggested that he give up Elvira.

"It's no good wandering around," said old Zompa. "The tree you uproot rarely gives off good fruit."

When we saw him coming back we thought it had all been a joke. But he had on his Sunday clothes and was carrying a bundle under his arm. Why had he come back?

"Now you need a passport to go to Rome!" shouted Berardo. "Every day they think up something new."

"Why?" asked Baldissera. "Isn't it part of Italy any more?"

Berardo's story was very confused.

"I was at the station," he said. "I had already bought my ticket. A squad of policemen came in and began asking for everybody's papers and about why we were traveling. I told them the truth, that I was going to Cammarese to work. They answered:

" 'Good! Do you have papers?'

" 'What papers?' I said.

" 'You can't work without papers.'

"I never could find out what kind of papers they

meant. They had the man give me back the price of the ticket and they sent me out of the station. Then I thought of walking to the next station and going from there. But again there were the policemen as soon as I had bought the ticket. Where was I going? To Cammarese to work. Then they said:

" 'Let's see your papers!'

" 'What papers? What have papers to do with it?'

" 'You can't work without papers. That's the new rule on internal emigration.' I tried to tell them that I wasn't going to Cammarese for internal emigration, but to find work. But it was useless.

" 'We have our orders,' they said. 'No worker can get on a train without papers if he's going somewhere else to work.'

"Again they had the man give me back the price of the ticket and again they sent me out of the station. I still couldn't understand what this papers business was all about. I went into an inn and started talking with the people who were there.

" 'Papers? Don't you know about papers?' said a carter to me. 'During the war all we talked about was papers.' And here I am again after having lost the whole day."

General Baldissera was the most moved by Berardo's story. He shuffled his old papers and came out with a printed folder.

"They talk about papers here too," he said, very much worried. As a matter of fact, the folder did talk about papers. The Federation of Artisans had peremptorily demanded that Baldissera get a cobbler's license.

"Elvira got one of those a few weeks ago!" Marietta said. "You can't work any more. They wrote that if she wants to keep on working she has to pay a fee and get a license."

This coincidence—that the letters had arrived at Fontamara at the same time that these things had happened to Berardo—made me think it was a joke.

"What has the government to do with cobblers and dyers?" I asked. "What does the government have to do with the peasants who go from one province to another looking for work? The government people have other things to worry about. Things like that go on only in wartime. But we're not at war."

"What do you know about that?" General Baldissera interrupted me. "How do you know whether we're at war or not?"

This got all of us worried.

"If the government requires you to have papers, it means we're at war," continued General Baldissera in a sad tone.

"Who is the war against?" asked Berardo. "Is it possible that we are at war without anyone knowing anything about it?"

"What do you know about it?" answered the General. "What business is it of yours, you ignorant and landless peasant? Peasants fight wars, but the authorities declare them. When the last war broke out, did anyone at Fontamara know whom it was against? Pilato thought it was against Emperor Menelik. Simpliciano thought it was against the Turks. Only much later we found out that it was against Trent and Trieste. But there have been wars where nobody knew whom we were fighting. A war is so complicated that a peasant can never understand it. A peasant sees a very small part of a war, like the papers, and this impresses him. The city man sees much more of it, like the barracks and the munitions factories. The king sees the whole country. Only God sees everything."

"Wars and epidemics," said Zompa, "were invented by governments to decrease the number of peasants. Now there must be too many of us again."

"But are you going to take out the license?" I asked Baldissera, to put an end to it.

"Of course I'll take out a license. But pay for it? You can be sure I won't pay for it!"

In spite of the different ways we said it, basically we meant the same thing when we spoke about permits.

That night a lot more was said about war. Most families were discussing it.

Everybody was asking everybody else:

"Whom is the war against?"

And nobody knew the answer. Seated in front of Marietta's place, General Baldissera patiently an-

swered everyone who came to ask questions. He
liked it.

"Whom is the war against? I don't know myself.
The paper doesn't say. It just says that you have to
pay for a license."

He said this to everyone.

"Paying. Always paying," said the peasants.

Things got even more confused with the unexpected arrival of Innocenzo La Legge.

There must have been a good reason for Innocenzo to come back to Fontamara, because he'd
been scared off for several months. He certainly
wouldn't have come there of his own accord. He
panicked for a minute when he saw everyone coming to him from all over. Marietta gave him a stool
before he collapsed.

"Excuse me!" he began in a tiny, hoarse voice.
"Don't be afraid! Do I scare you?"

"Talk," said Berardo in an encouraging tone.

"Ah . . . let's get things straight," Innocenzo
continued. "There's no new tax. I swear it on all the
Saints! . . . There's nothing to pay! If there's a
tax, may God blind me!"

There was a slight pause, just long enough for
God to think the matter over. Innocenzo kept his
sight.

"Keep talking!" ordered Berardo.

"Er . . . ah . . . you remember the night
that militia veteran came here? . . . Cavaliere
Pelino? You remember him? . . . Good! . . .

Fine! . . . That's excellent! . . . Well, Cavaliere Pelino has reported to the higher authorities that Fontamara is a nest of enemies of the present government. Don't get alarmed. There's nothing to worry about. The Cavaliere has noted, word for word, some of the things that were said in his presence against the present government and the Church. Surely he misunderstood what you said. I assure you it's nothing serious, nothing to pay, nothing at all. Just some petty details which are important in the city but which any sensible peasant knows enough not to worry about."

Innocenzo didn't know all of what had been decided about Fontamara. He was just the town messenger and of what had been decided he knew only that which he was supposed to tell other people. The rest he didn't know. And he cared less. The first decision was about the re-establishment in the village of Fontamara of the old curfew law: no peasant could be out of his house an hour after vespers, and he had to stay home until dawn.

"And will the pay be the same?" Berardo asked.

"What does the pay have to do with it?" Innocenzo said.

"What do you mean what does it have to do with it? If we can't get out of the house before dawn, that means that we'll get to Fucino where we work a little before noon. If they'll give us the same pay for a couple of hours' work, hurrah for the curfew!"

"And the irrigation?" asked Pilato. "How can

we run the irrigation at night if we have to stay at home?"

Innocenzo La Legge was speechless.

"You don't understand!" he said. "Or maybe you're pretending you don't understand, just to give me difficulty. Who said you had to change your ways? You are peasants and should do things the way you like. But the Trader is podestà and you can't keep him from being podestà. And what am I? Just the town messenger. The Trader, as podestà, decides to protect himself from the higher authorities, so he orders you to stay home at night. I'm the messenger and I just bring you the order. You peasants do as you like."

"And what about the law?" yelled General Baldissera. "Where is the law going to end up? Is there law or isn't there?"

"What time do you go to bed?" asked Innocenzo.

"As soon as it's dark," answered the half-blind old shoemaker.

"And what time do you get up in the morning?"

"At ten, because there's not much work—and I'm old and tired."

"Excellent!" said the messenger. "I appoint you the custodian of this law."

We all burst out laughing. But Baldissera was gloomy, and since it was already dusk, he went off to bed.

Innocenzo was delighted at the unexpected success and the mirth. He relaxed a little. He lit up a cigarette and began smoking. But he smoked in a strange way. Instead of blowing the smoke out of his mouth, he kept it in and blew it out of his nostrils, not from both of them (even we can do that), but first from one, then from the other.

He took advantage of his momentary popularity to tell us of the second decision about Fontamara. All the public places had to have a sign saying:

IN THIS PLACE NO POLITICAL
DISCUSSIONS ARE ALLOWED.

Marietta's was the only public place in all Fontamara. Innocenzo gave her a piece of paper with an order from the podestà that she would be held responsible if any political discussions were held in her wineshop.

"But nobody at Fontamara knows anything about politics," said Marietta. And she was right. "Nobody ever talked politics in my place."

"Then what was Cavaliere Pelino so angry about when he went back to the city?" asked Innocenzo with a smile.

"We talked a bit about everything," continued Marietta. "We talked about prices, salaries, taxes and laws. Today we were talking about licenses, war and emigration."

"But according to the podestà's order, you shouldn't talk about these things," said Innocenzo. "This isn't just for Fontamara. It's for all of Italy.

You can't talk about prices, taxes, wages or laws in public places."

"In other words, you can't argue," concluded Berardo.

"Exactly! Berardo understood perfectly!" exclaimed Innocenzo. "You can't argue any more; this is the gist of the podestà's order. No more arguments. And then, what good are arguments anyway? If you're hungry, can you eat arguments? We have to get rid of these useless things."

Innocenzo's satisfaction was great when Berardo agreed with him, so he consented to make the sign on the wall clearer, and he himself scribbled, in our presence, on a large piece of paper the following:

BY ORDER OF THE PODESTÀ
THERE WILL BE NO MORE ARGUING.

Berardo had the sign put up in front of the wine-shop in a high place. We were amazed at his good humor. As if his attitude were't already clear enough, Berardo added:

"Don't anybody touch this sign!"

Innocenzo shook his hand and wanted to embrace him.

But Berardo's explanations, soon given, moderated La Legge's enthusiasm.

"I have always said what the podestà has ordered today. There's no sense arguing with the landlords. That's my rule. All the peasant's trouble comes from arguing. A peasant is an arguing donkey, so our life is a hundred times worse than that of the real donkeys, who don't argue (or at least pretend they can't). The unreasoning donkey carries a hundred and fifty, two hundred or even two hundred and fifty pounds—and no more. The unreasoning donkey needs a certain amount of hay. You can't get from him what you get from a cow or from a goat or from a horse. No amount of arguing will convince him. He doesn't understand you, or pretends he doesn't. But the peasant argues. He can be persuaded. He can be persuaded to go without food. He can be persuaded to support the landlord. He can be persuaded to go off to war. He can be persuaded that in the next world there's a hell, even if he hasn't seen it. You see what happens. Just take a look around!"

This was no news to us. But Innocenzo La Legge was terrified.

"An unreasoning being won't go without food. He says, 'If I eat I can work; if I don't eat, I can't work.' Or better yet, he doesn't say so, because then he would be thinking. But that's the way he acts. Just think what it would be like if the eight thousand men who cultivate Fucino, instead of being reasoning donkeys—that is, housebroken, tractable, afraid of the policemen, the priest, the judge, and so on—were real donkeys, totally devoid of reason? Prince Torlonia might have to go begging.

You came here, Innocenzo, and in a little while you'll be going back to the city by a dark road. What's to prevent us from killing you? Answer!"

Innocenzo was about to stammer something, but he couldn't. He was white as a sheet.

"I'll tell you what could prevent it," continued Berardo. "Arguing about the possible consequences of the murder would prevent it. But you, Innocenzo, with your own hands, have written out on that sign that beginning today by order of the podestà all arguing is forbidden. You have broken the thread your safety hung by."

"Well! You say you're against arguing," Innocenzo managed to say, "but it seems to me . . . that is . . . the way I look at it, everything you've said is a great big argument. I never heard a donkey—that is, an unreasoning peasant—talk like that."

"If arguing is only good for the landlords and the authorities," I asked Berardo, "why has the podestà forbidden all arguing?"

Berardo didn't say anything for a minute, then he answered:

"It's late. Tomorrow I have to get up at three to go to Fucino. Good night!"

And he went home.

And that was the way most arguments with him ended up. He talked and shouted for hours on end like a preacher, saying the stupidest and most violent things as they came into his head and in a tone that allowed for no back talk. Then when he was through, and someone asked him a question that embarrassed him, he went off without saying anything.

Innocenzo La Legge stayed at Fontamara that evening. Perhaps because of Berardo's rough talk, or perhaps because of some sudden weakness, he preferred to spend the night at Marietta's place. I must add that this was not the first time he had done so. As a matter of fact, we used to say to each other:

"They could get married. Why don't they get married?"

"If I get married," Marietta explained, "I lose my pension as the Widow of the Dead Hero. That's the way the law is."

And some men thought she was right, but not the women.

4.

Toward the end of June word got around that the representatives of the peasants of Marsica were to be called to a great reunion at Avezzano to hear the decisions of the new government at Rome on the Fucino question.

The news, which Berardo so hopefully brought us, seemed strange, for the previous governments had never wanted to admit that there was such a thing as the Fucino question, and since the end of the elections don Circostanza himself had forgotten all about this matter that had once been the topic of so many of his speeches. But there certainly was no doubt about the new government at Rome, because we had been hearing about that for a long time. This seemed to mean that there had been war, or that there was going to be one, since only a war could throw out a government and impose a new one. Where we live, as the old people tell us, the Bourbons had taken the place of the Spaniards, and the Piedmontese that of the Bourbons. But as yet nobody knew what sort of people the new rulers were or what country they came from.

When there is a new government, a poor peasant can do nothing but say:

"May God send us a good one!"

Just as when in summer great clouds appear on the horizon, it's not the peasant's business to decide whether they will pour down water or hail, but the Eternal Father's. However, it still seemed funny that a representative of the new government wanted to talk face-to-face with a peasant. We were pretty incredulous. But not General Baldissera.

"The old law has come back," he explained. "When there were no barracks between the court and the peasants' huts, none of the prefectures and subprefectures we have now, the rulers put on peasants' clothes once a year and went to the fairs to hear what the poor people were complaining about. Then came the elections, and the rulers lost sight of the poor people. But now, if what they say is true, we're going back to the old law, which never should have been abandoned in the first place."

Michele Zompa had the same faith, for different reasons:

"A government made with elections is always controlled by the rich, because they run the elections," he said. "But if just one man runs the whole government, he can frighten the rich. Could there be jealousy or competition between a ruler and a peasant? It would be ridiculous. But it would be easy between a ruler and Prince Torlonia."

The hope of getting some land from a division at Fucino prevented Berardo from contradicting everyone's opinions, as was otherwise his custom and vice.

"All governments are made up of thieves," he said. "Naturally it's better for the peasants if the government is made up of just one thief, rather than five hundred, because a big thief, no matter how big he is, always eats less than five hundred little ones. If they're going to divide up the land at Fucino, Fontamara will have to speak up for its rights."

At this imminent possibility, Berardo was overcome by an orgasmic emotion that he couldn't hold back. And he could speak of nothing else.

"The land at Fucino is the promised land!" he said. "There you harvest ten bags of grain for every one planted. It's good, fat land with no stones. And it's level, safe from floods!"

But who didn't know this? And we also knew that Fontamara, a village in the mountains, had never been given the rights of the villages on the bank of the lake, and therefore had been excluded from the use of bottom lands when the land was drained.

"Excluded!" exclaimed Berardo. "But when there was all that work to be done, we went to Fucino too!"

"As day laborers," said Zompa, "not as tenants. Would you claim land in the king's garden if you'd worked there for a day?"

"And why can't they rent us land if they need us as day laborers?" replied Berardo, shaking his fist.

For years Fontamara had begged for this right, but they had always laughed at us. "You're mountain people," they said. "If you want land, go look for it in the mountains."

But one Sunday morning a truck came to Fontamara with a devil of a noise. It stopped in the middle of the square, and a fellow in uniform got out and began shouting to the ones who gathered around it:

"Avezzano! We're going to Avezzano! Get in!" And he pointed to the truck.

"How much is it?" asked old Zompa.

"It's free!" the driver explained. "The round trip is free. Get in! Get in! Get in quickly or we'll all be late!"

"Free?" Zompa curled his lip and shook his head.

"Maybe you'd rather pay," said the driver.

"No!" Zompa quickly exclaimed. "May God deliver us from that! But if there's nothing to pay, it's a swindle."

The driver didn't pay any more attention to him, and started yelling again:

"Hurry up! First come, first served!"

Berardo ran up and without a word—on the contrary, with a joy none of us had ever seen in him before—jumped onto the truck.

After that there was no more dawdling, but we were still a bit dubious. There happened to be about ten of us in the village that day. The rest of us were in the fields, because in the summer when there's lots to be done even the Church lets us work on Sundays. But none of us could blame the government for not knowing that there was a harvest at the end of June. How can the government know when the harvest is?

On the other hand, it would be stupid, for the sake of a day's work, to miss a meeting where the Fucino question was to be resolved, perhaps in our favor.

All of a sudden the old hope rose up in us again: the good, fat land on the plains that don Circostanza had told us so much about (especially just before elections). "Fucino must be given to the peasants who work it" was don Circostanza's slogan. "Fucino must be taken from the prince and the false tenants, rich farmers, lawyers, and other professional people, and given to the ones who work it—that is, the peasants."

For this reason, we were all very excited as we got into the truck at the idea that at Avezzano that very day there was to be a division of the lands, and that the government had sent the truck because it wanted the peasants to have their part. The few of us who were there got on quickly without asking for any explanations. There were Berardo Viola, Antonio La Zappa, Della Croce, Baldovino, Simplicio, Giacobbe, Pilato and his son Caporale, Scamorza and I. We were sorry not even to have time to change our shirts, but the driver kept yelling at us to hurry up.

But before we left, right at the last minute, he asked us:

"Where's your banner?"

"What banner?" we asked.

"My orders say that every group of farmers absolutely must have a banner," the driver added.

"But what is a banner?" we asked, embarrassed.

"A banner is a flag," explained the driver, laughing.

We didn't want to make a bad impression on the government at a ceremony where the Fucino question was to be settled. So we accepted the proposal of Teofilo, who held the keys of the church and who thought of taking along San Rocco's banner. He went to the church with Scamorza to get it, but when the driver saw them coming, holding aloft with the utmost difficulty a thirty-foot pole to which was attached a huge blue-and-white banner of San Rocco with a picture of the dog licking his wounds, he was against bringing it in the truck. But we haven't any other flag at Fontamara, and on Berardo's insistence, the driver consented to bring it along.

"It'll make it all the funnier," he said.

To hold it up in the moving truck we had to take turns three at a time, and it was very hard. Our standard was more like the mast of a storm-tossed ship than a flag. It must have been visible for quite a distance, because we saw the peasants who were working in the various fields making amazed gestures, while the women knelt and crossed themselves.

The truck went crazily down the hill with little attention to the curves, and we were tossed about like cattle on a train. But we laughed at it. Even the unusual speed gave our trip the character of an extraordinary adventure. But when we came, after the last curve, to the plain of Fucino, emotion took our breath away. Fucino looked new. It looked like the promised land. At this point Berardo picked up the standard himself, and with the force of emotion waved the picture of the holy pilgrim and the pious dog high in the air.

"Land! Land!" he yelled, as if he had never seen any before.

As we came into the first village on the way to the plain, the driver told us:

"Sing the anthem!"

"What anthem?" we asked, embarrassed.

"My orders say that when crossing every inhabited locality the farmers are to sing the anthem and give signs of enthusiasm," the driver answered.

But we didn't know any anthem, and furthermore we were already part of a large procession consisting of numerous cars and motorcycles, together with patrician buggies and plebeian trucks, all of which were going in the same direction. All these people were at first surprised at our huge blue-and-white standard; they just roared with laughter. The flags they had were black and no bigger than a handkerchief. Each had a skull and crossbones in the middle, like that you'd see on a telephone pole where it says "Danger." In other words, there was nothing as good as ours.

"Are they the living-deads?" asked Baldovino, pointing to the men with the funereal banners. "Are they the souls don Circostanza bought?"

"They're the souls the government bought," explained Berardo.

Coming into Avezzano, we had a fight over the flag. In the middle of the street we ran into a group of boys who were waiting just for us. They told us to hand it over. We refused because we didn't have anything else. The driver was told to stop the truck and the boys tried to force us to give it up. But we were fed up with everybody's making fun of us, so we fought back. A lot of their black shirts got gray from the dust on the road.

A great howling mob gathered around the truck. There were a lot of boys in black shirts, but also many peasants from the villages around Fontamara who recognized us and shouted greetings. We kept silent and stood in the truck, determined not to put up with any more insults. Suddenly the sweaty, fat, puffing figure of don Abbacchio showed up in the middle of the crowd, together with some policemen. None of us doubted that as a priest he would come to the defense of San Rocco. But he didn't.

"What do you think this is, carnival?" he began shouting at us. "Is this how you compromise the pact between the authorities and the Church? When are you ever going to stop these stupidities?"

Without another word we let the boys in black shirts take our standard. Berardo was the first to give in. If a priest was going to betray San Rocco, why should we keep faith with him at the risk of our rights to Fucino?

We were taken to a great square where we were given a good place in the shade behind the court-house. Other groups of peasants were placed near the various buildings in the square. Between the groups there were patrols of policemen. Little groups of them on bicycles were crossing the square in all directions. As soon as a new truck arrived, the peasants were taken off by the policemen and shown to their places in the square. It looked as if they were getting ready for something important. At one point a police officer crossed the square on a horse. Berardo thought it was a very handsome horse, and we all admired it in great ecstasy.

Right after that a messenger arrived and handed an order to the patrols. Berardo pointed out how efficient it all was. One policeman came out of his group and gave the peasants an order:

"You may sit on the ground."

We stayed there on the ground about an hour. After we had waited that hour, the arrival of a new group of policemen was greeted with a tremendous roar. Some authorities arrived from a corner of the square. The policemen ordered us:

"Get up! Get up! Yell with all your might:

" 'Hurrah for the podestà! Hurrah for the honest administrators! Hurrah for the administrators-who-don't-rob!' "

The only one of the administrators-who-don't-rob whom we recognized was the Trader. After the administrators-who-don't-rob had gone by we sat down on the ground again—by permission of the police. Berardo began to get bored with the ceremonies.

"And the land?" he asked some of the policemen. "When are they going to talk about the land?"

After a few minutes there was another procession and more cheering.

"Get up! Get up!" ordered the policemen. "Yell: 'Hurrah for the prefect!' "

The prefect passed by in a shining automobile, and then we could sit on the ground again—by permission of the police.

But as soon as we were seated, the policemen made us get up again.

"Yell as loud as you can:
'Hurrah for the minister!' "

At that moment a huge car appeared, followed by four men on bicycles, and it went rapidly by as we cheered at the top of our lungs:

"Hurrah for the minister!"

Then we sat down again—by permission of the police. The policemen began eating their rations in shifts. We opened our knapsacks and began eating the bread we had brought from home.

"Now the minister will call us," Berardo kept saying. "You'll see. They're studying our case and they'll call us in a minute. Let's eat quickly."

But about two the whole business started up again. The minister passed first, then the prefect, then the administrators-who-don't-rob. Each time we had to get up and give signs of enthusiasm. And at the end the policeman said to us:

"Dismissed! You may go!"

They had to explain it more clearly.

"The festival is over. You may go or you may visit Avezzano. But you have only an hour. You have to go in an hour."

"And the minister? And the Fucino question?" we asked in amazement. Nobody would listen to us. But we couldn't just stay there without having concluded anything and without having understood what went on.

"Come with me!" said Berardo, who knew Avezzano from having been there in jail.

His tone had changed.

"Maybe I'll go back to jail," he told us. "But I've got to find out. Come with me."

We came to a palace that was all covered with flags.

"We want to speak with the minister!" barked Berardo at the policeman who was guarding the door.

The policeman pounced on Berardo as if he had uttered the most horrible blasphemy. But we came to his aid and there was a fight. From the inside of the palace there came a whole crowd of people, among them don Circostanza, evidently drunk, with his trousers at the third stage.

"Let no one lack respect for my Fontamarans!" he shouted. "Treat my Fontamarans well!"

The policeman let us alone and don Circostanza came to us. He wanted to kiss everyone in the group and he was particularly affectionate with Berardo.

"We want to speak with the minister," we said to the People's Friend.

"I'm afraid the minister's already gone," he answered. "Urgent business, you know, an affair of state."

"We want to know what happened with the Fucino question!" Berardo drily interrupted.

Don Circostanza had a policeman take us to the Prince's administrative offices, and there we found a clerk who patiently explained to us how the Fucino question had been settled.

"Has the new government taken up the question of Fucino?" asked Berardo.

"Yes, and satisfactorily to all," answered the clerk, with a false smile.

"Why didn't they call us for the discussion? Why did they leave us out in the square?" protested Pilato. "Aren't we Christians too?"

"The minister couldn't talk with ten thousand people. But he has discussed the matter with your representatives," the clerk replied. "Be reason-able."

"Who's our representative?" I asked.

"The Cavaliere Pelino, a veteran of the militia," he answered.

"How was the land divided? How much does Fontamara get? When's the division going to be?" Berardo insisted impatiently.

"The land isn't going to be divided," the clerk said. "The minister and the peasants' representa-tives have decided, on the contrary, that the small tenants should if possible be eliminated. Many of them got their land because they were in the war, but that wasn't fair."

"Exactly!" said Berardo rudely. "You don't know how to work land just because you've been in war. The important thing is to work the land. Let's give Fucino to the people who work it. That's what don Circostanza's always said. At Fontamara——"

"That's the minister's idea also," continued the clerk, smiling the false smile again. "Let's give Fucino to the people who work it. Let's give Fucino to those who have the means to cultivate it—or have it cultivated. In other words, to those with suffi-cient capital. Fucino must be liberated from the small tenants and given to the rich farmers. Those without capital have no right to rent land at Fucino. Have you anything else to ask?"

He explained all that to us in the same tone of voice he would use if we had asked what time it was.

His face was impassive as a clock's.

"Everything is perfectly clear," we answered.

Everything was perfectly clear. The streets were full of lights. It had gotten late, but the streets were as light as day. (Everything was perfectly clear.) But what was it all about? I was asking myself. Avezzano looked as if it were going mad. The way the people worked at their singing and dancing, it was hard for me to believe and made me feel funny. I wondered if it were all a joke. Or had they all gone crazy without knowing it?

"The city people are having a good time!" said Berardo. "The city people are really enjoying themselves. They're eating. Right in front of the peasants!"

A party of drunken young gentlemen passed us, singing to the accompaniment of obscene gestures:

> *With a mixture of hair,*
> *We'll make a fine pair . . .*

A man without arms or legs, pulled on a little cart by a dog, came rapidly up to the group to beg.

A second party, which contained the boys in black shirts who had taken our standard from us when we got there, followed on the first. As soon as they saw us they yelled with an ugly noise:

"Right in San Rocco's face!" Then they joined hands and formed a circle around us and began jumping about, singing a filthy song with obscene gestures, which parodied the act of love. The song ran:

> *Though it's not in good taste,*
> *We'll join at the waist . . .*

We let them. Nobody felt like doing anything about it. We didn't understand any more. We were stunned and depressed.

The boys left us.

"You're too stupid!" they told us. "You're no fun at all!"

Their hilarity was disgusting. Berardo was exasperated and was about to grab one of them and beat him up.

"Not now! Not now!" I begged him, taking him by the arm. "It'll be the end of you. Don't you see the policemen?"

Then we remembered the truck that was supposed to take us back to Fontamara, and we went to the place where the driver had told us to meet for the return trip.

"Your truck has already gone!" a mechanic yelled at us. "Why are you so late?"

And he began to make fun of us, as if we were stupid and childish. But the idea of having to go back to Fontamara on foot made us so discouraged that we were indifferent to all further insults. We hung around the garage door like a herd of sheep with no sheep dog.

A gentleman whom we had observed following us for quite some time came up to us. He was well dressed and I remember that he had red hair, a red mustache and a scar on his chin.

"Are you from Fontamara?" he asked us. "Do you know that the authorities are afraid of you? The authorities know that you are against the new government."

We let him talk. We had other things to worry about.

"But you're right," he continued. "You are right to rebel. We can't get anything done this way. Come with me where we can talk."

The gentleman led us through a side street. And we followed him like sheep. A young man in clothes halfway between a worker's and a student's followed behind and smiled at us two or three times as if he had something to tell us. The gentleman with the red hair went into an obscure and deserted wineshop. We went in after him. The young man, who had followed us, hesitated a bit, then came in and went to sit at a table near ours.

The redheaded man ordered some wine and gave the young man a dirty look. Then in a low voice he took up what he'd been saying on the street.

"You can't get anything done this way. The peasants have stood all they can. You people are ignorant. You need an educated person to lead you. Don Circostanza has spoken very highly of you. He likes you, but he is prudent. He doesn't like to compromise himself. If you need me, I am at your disposal. If you have any plans, ask my advice. Understand?"

The way this man put himself at our disposal would have seemed suspicious to anyone who wasn't in our state of mind. This was the first time that a city man had talked to us like that. We let him talk.

"I understand you. All I have to do is look you in the eye and I understand you," he went on. "The police told you that you must leave Avezzano in an hour, and the hour is gone and you're still here. I understand you. You want to do something against the authorities. That's obvious; you can't deny it. And why am I here? I am here to help you, to give you advice, to sacrifice myself with you. Understand?"

But we really didn't understand. Pilato was about to say something, but Berardo signaled him to be quiet.

"All right," continued the stranger. "I'm an enemy of the government too. Maybe you want to say to me, 'Yes, we want to do something against the authorities, but we have no means, no arms.' It's easy. Nothing could be easier."

We hadn't said a word, but the city man kept right on talking all by himself. He asked questions and gave the answers.

"You could say to me, 'These are words, but the facts are harder.' All right, try me. If you wait here for me fifteen minutes, I'll bring you what you want and I'll tell you how to use it. Do you have any doubts? Don't you believe me? Wait for me here!"

He got up, shook hands with all of us, paid for the wine he had ordered, and left.

As soon as he had gone, the young man who was seated at the next table came to us and said:

"That man is a policeman. He's an *agent provocateur*. Watch out. He'll bring you some dynamite, then have you arrested. Go away before he gets back!"

We left Avezzano by way of the fields to avoid meeting the *agent provocateur*. But the young man who had warned us against him didn't want to leave us, and he kept on mumbling incredible stories to us until Berardo got sick of it and after twice having told him to go away, picked him up and dumped him in a ditch.

Thirsty, hungry, and with gall in our souls, we walked all the way back along the road over which we had so hopefully come in the truck that morning with the banner of San Rocco unfurled to the wind.

We got back to Fontamara around midnight, in what condition I leave you to imagine. At three the next morning we had to get up and go to the fields, because it was harvesttime.

5.

The town had built a wooden fence around the pasture land that the Trader had appropriated without payment.

The fence was to put an end to all the peasants' chatter about the fact that for thousands of years the land had been owned in common. But the discussions continued. One night the fence burned up.

"The wood was too dry," explained Berardo. "The sun burned it."

"More likely the light of the moon," I corrected. "It burned up at night."

The Trader had another fence built at the town's expense and put an armed street cleaner on guard over it. Could a street cleaner bring fear to this meadow that since the beginning of time had seen every variety of wolf, shepherd's squabble, brigand, war and invasion?

The fence burned up right under the street cleaner's nose. He distinctly saw bursts of flame come out of the earth and ignite the whole fence in a very few minutes. As is obligatory for every miracle, the street cleaner told don Abbacchio all about it, then everyone else who would listen. Don Abbacchio established that the fire was of undoubted supernatural origin, but of diabolic initiative. And we discovered that the Devil wasn't as bad as he was cracked up to be after all. But the Trader, who had to rescue the prestige of authority and who couldn't arrest the Devil, had the street cleaner locked up.

"Who will win?" we asked ourselves. "The Devil or the Trader?" (We were all against the Trader, but the only open partisan of the Devil was Berardo.)

One evening at dusk some of us women were talking about this on the square while we were waiting for our men to come back from Fucino. Maria Grazia, Ciammaruga, Filomena Castagna, Recchiuta and Cannarozzo's daughter were there with me, and we were as usual sitting on the little wall by the square that faces the valley. We were looking toward the plain, which was already submerged in shadow. The valley below Fontamara, divided into two parts by the dusty national highway, seemed silent and deserted. The road that rises from the plain to Fontamara, curling back and forth on the hill, was also deserted and silent. Our men were supposed to come back late; you don't work regular hours during the harvest. I also remember that Maria Christina was in a corner of the square, wearing black for the recent death of her husband. She was winnowing the few grains of maize that had been gathered from her field, letting them fall from the pan she held high against the wind.

Nobody had any idea of what was about to happen and we were talking of everyday things.

"What will we give our men next winter, if the drought kills all our beans?"

"And what will we plant in the fall," said Filomena, "if we have to eat up all the seed corn?"

"This will pass by, God willing, as a lot of other things have passed by," said the trusting Recchiuta. "How many times have we said that things can't go on like this, and they went on like that anyway?"

In a corner of the square some of the children were playing sheriff. The sheriff couldn't go on foot. He had to ride a horse, and each little girl had to take her turn at being the horse. Then the sun set and the first fireflies came out. A little girl (I think it was one of Maria Christina's) came to ask me if it were true that the fireflies were looking for little pieces of grain to feed the hungry souls in Purgatory, and she had a few pieces of grain in her hand.

Meanwhile, without any of us being immediately aware of it, a monotonous sound began to work its way into the silence. At first it was like a beehive, then like a threshing machine. It came out of the valley, but there was no telling what it was. There weren't any threshing machines and the threshing grounds were empty. Besides, the threshing machines didn't come up out of the valley except at the end of the harvest. All of a sudden it became distinct, and on the first curve on the road leading up from the plain, there appeared a truck full of people. Right behind it came another. And another.

Five trucks, all coming to Fontamara. But there came still another. Were there ten, twelve, fifteen of them? Cannarozzo's daughter shouted that there were a hundred, but she couldn't count. The first was already at the last curve coming into Fontamara, and the last was still at the foot of the hill. We had never seen so many trucks before. None of us had ever imagined that there could be so many trucks.

Alarmed by the unfamiliar roar of so many machines, the entire population of Fontamara had assembled in the square, in front of the church: women, children and the old men who hadn't gone off to the fields. Everyone had his own explanation for the unexpected arrival of so many machines at Fontamara.

"It's a pilgrimage!" yelled Marietta, all excited. "Now the rich pilgrims don't go on foot, but in cars. It's probably a pilgrimage for our San Rocco."

"But today isn't San Rocco's day!" I said.

"Maybe it's the auto race," said Cipolla, who had done his military service in the city. "It's a race to see who goes the farthest. In the city there are automobile races every day."

The noise of the trucks got louder and more terrifying. This was soon heightened by the savage cries of the men on them. A burst of gunfire, followed by the fall of glass from the church windows, changed our curiosity into panic.

"They're shooting at us! They're shooting at the church!" we screamed.

"Get back! Get back!" shouted Baldissera to us women who were closest to the parapet. "Get back! They're shooting at us!"

"But who are they? Why are they shooting at us?"

"It's the war! It's the war!" said Baldissera exultantly.

"But why is there a war and why is it against us?"

"It's a war!" repeated Baldissera. "God only knows why there's a war."

"If there's a war, we'll have to repeat the litanies of war," said Teofilo the sacristan, and he had begun repeating, *Regina pacis, ora pro nobis*, when a second burst of rifle fire riddled the front of the church and covered us with rubble.

The litanies were shattered. Everything that followed was absolutely senseless. War? But why was there a war? Giuditta was seized with convulsions. We were like a herd of maddened goats around her. Only Baldissera remained grave and inscrutable.

"There's nothing to be done!" he said. "It's war! There's nothing to do! It's fate! This is how all wars begin!"

Maria Rosa, Berardo's mother, had a good idea.

"Let's ring the church bells. When the village is in danger, we've always rung the church bells."

But Teofilo was too scared to do anything. He gave me the keys. Elvira, who had just then come out onto the square, went with me to ring the church bells. But when we got there she hesitated a moment and asked:

"Have there ever been wars against women?"

"Not that I've ever heard of," I answered.

"Look," she said. "These people have come for the men, not for us. It would be better not to give out the alarm. If we ring the bells, the men will think there's a fire and come back and run into these people."

Elvira was certainly thinking of Berardo. I thought of my husband and son. We stayed in the church tower without ringing the bells.

From the tower we saw the trucks stopping at the entrance to Fontamara and large numbers of men armed with rifles getting off. Some stayed with the trucks, and the others set off in the direction of the church.

At our feet the women, children and old people had finished reciting the litanies and were beginning on the exorcisms. Teofilo the sacristan, with a trembling voice, recited the invocation and the others answered in chorus: *Libera nos, Domine.* Elvira and I also answered, kneeling and in a low voice: *Libera nos, Domine.* Nobody knew what was going to happen. Teofilo went through the list of all possible exorcisms, and each one of us added: *Libera nos, Domine.*

From every evil, deliver us, O Lord,
From every sin, deliver us, O Lord,

From Thine own anger, deliver us, O Lord,
From sudden and unforeseen death, deliver
* us, O Lord,*
A spiritu fornicationis, libera nos, Domine.

No one could imagine what horrible things were going to happen. Teofilo had come to the exorcism against pestilence, famine and war when the column of armed men emerged onto the square, yelling and waving their guns about. We were terrified by so many men. Elvira and I instinctively drew back into a corner of the church tower so we could continue to see without being seen.

There were probably two hundred of them. In addition to a rifle, each of them carried a knife on his belt. They all had masks bearing the skull and crossbones. We were able to recognize for certain only the local policeman and Filippo il Bello, the roadman. But the rest of them were familiar enough. They looked a little like peasants, but landless ones, the peasants who enter the service of the landlords, earning little and living mostly from thievery and on jail food. Some of them, we learned later, were smalltime merchants (the ones you see at the markets), dishwashers, barbers, private coachmen and wandering musicians. Lazy people who are cowardly by day. People who are obsequious toward the landlords on the condition that they may do as they like with the poor. People with no scruples. People who once came to us to bring us don Circostanza's orders for the elections and now came with rifles to make war on us. They were people without family, without honor, without faith, untrustworthy people, poor yet the enemies of the poor.

Their leader was a little potbellied man with a tricolor on his stomach. Filippo was strutting along beside him.

"What are you doing?" asked the potbellied little man of Teofilo the sacristan.

"I'm praying for peace," said the frightened man of the church.

"I'll give you peace all right," the potbelly added, laughing. He signaled to Filippo il Bello.

The roadman came up to Teofilo, and after some hesitation, hit him.

Teofilo put his hand on the cheek that had been struck and asked timidly:

"But why?"

"Coward! Coward!" the man with the three-colored belly said reproachfully. "Why don't you hit him back? Coward!"

But Teofilo didn't move a muscle or say a word. More than anything else he was surprised. In all this crowd of women, children, old people and invalids, the potbellied man couldn't have found anyone else less likely to hit back. He consulted a little with Filippo and said with contempt:

"It doesn't look as if we could do anything about it."

Then he turned to the crowd and ordered in a strident voice:

"Go home, all of you!"

When no more of the villagers were on the square, the little man turned to the men in black and ordered:

"Split into fives and go into every house! Search everywhere and confiscate every type of arms! Quick, before the men get back!"

The little square was empty in no time. It had got dark. But from our refuge we could see the patrols of five go off into the little streets and the houses.

"It will be hard to search all the houses without light!" I said.

"My father is in bed and he'll be frightened. I'd better go home and light the lamp," said Elvira, getting ready to come down from the church tower.

"No! Stay here!" I said to her. "They won't do anything to your father!"

"But what sort of arms are they looking for?" asked Elvira. "We haven't any rifles. It's lucky that Berardo is in the fields!"

"They'll take away the rakes and the sickles," I said. "We haven't anything else."

But a sudden yell from Maria Grazia, whose house was right next to the church tower, and the desperate cries of Filomena Castagna and Carracina, and other yells from houses that were farther off, accompanied by the sound of overturned furniture, broken chairs and shattered glass, told us at once just what those sons of bitches were after.

Just below us Maria Grazia was screaming like a stuck pig. Through the wide-open door we saw the confused tussle of five men with the poor woman. Several times she was able to free herself, and once she got as far as the door. But she was taken back in time and held by the shoulders and the legs, was thrown on the ground and pinned down, stripped of everything she had on and held by four men, with her arms wide open and her legs wide apart, so the fifth could rape her. Maria Grazia's scream was like the death rattle of a slaughtered animal. When the first one was through with her, his place was taken by another and the martyrdom continued. Finally she gave up all resistance; her cries were so weak that we couldn't hear them any more.

Elvira, who was right next to me, had seen the whole thing. How could I have prevented it? It had all happened right under our noses, just a few yards away. The poor girl clung to me and trembled as if she were seized with convulsions. It was as if the entire church tower and all the earth under it were trembling. I did my best to hold up Elvira, to prevent her from falling downstairs and revealing our hiding place to the armed men. With enormous wide-open and immobile eyes, Elvira regarded the room from which the five men had come out and where lay the lacerated body of Maria Grazia. I was afraid that Elvira was going mad.

I closed her eyes with my hands, the way you do with the dead. Then all of a sudden I weakened too; my legs collapsed, and we both fainted and fell side by side.

I don't remember anything else of that horrible evening except what I have tried to tell you about. Sometimes I can't remember anything else about my whole life except what went on that evening, what I've just told you about.

If you like, my husband can tell you the rest.

We men, who were coming back from Fucino, couldn't have know anything about all this. (If only they had rung the bells!) Some of us, including Berardo, had met on the road and were coming back together. Some of the others were close behind us. When we saw the long line of trucks and the group of soldiers at the entrance to the village, Berardo said:

"It must be about the fence! The Trader must think that someone from Fontamara has burned his fence. Whatever can have given him such an idea?"

Some of the soldiers who were guarding the trucks knew Berardo personally and were afraid of him. When he came they got awfully scared, but they didn't want to explain to us why they had come to Fontamara, or maybe they didn't know themselves. They just told us to wait, and when the second group of peasants arrived, they took us into

Fontamara, to the square, and there we found the rest of the soldiers arranged in squares and commanded by a little potbellied man with a three-colored badge on his stomach. He was assisted by Filippo il Bello. To our great surprise, we found Baldissera, Teofilo the sacristan, Cipolla, old Braciola, Anacleto the tailor, and some others, the ones who hadn't gone to work in the fields. They were mute, immobile, pale—as resigned as prisoners of war.

"What's happening?" asked Berardo. But nobody answered.

When we arrived, the formation opened and closed up again after we went in. Berardo looked at me, not knowing whether to be amused or angry. We tried to find out from Baldissera a little of what could have happened before we had come back. He came up to me and whispered into my ear:

"Nothing like this ever happened before!" And then he came to Berardo and repeated in his ear the same words, then he came to the others and murmured the same words in their ears: "Nothing like this ever happened before! Not ever!"

This, perhaps, was not completely clear, but it was nevertheless extraordinary, because up to that moment Baldissera had always had some precedent in local history for even the strangest things that went on. For the first time he had admitted to us that he didn't understand.

The formation of soldiers opened once again to

admit and surround a third group of men who had come back from work. Among them were Pilato, Losurdo, Michele Zompa, Testone, Uliva, Gasparone, and some of the boys. They looked at us as if we were responsible for everything, but with all those armed men around, not even they dared to protest.

"When things get out of order," said Zompa to me, "who is to put them right?"

I was pleading with Berardo to keep still, not even to whisper, not to compromise us all, to do by himself whatever stupid things he wanted to do, and to do them later if he had to do them, but not in front of all those rifles.

After that some of the others came to keep us company. Maria Grazia's fiancé was among them. No one understood what was happening. Nobody spoke. Everybody looked at his neighbor. We all knew that we were dealing with the authorities for some reason or other, and nobody was going to compromise himself more than the others. Every once in a while more people would arrive. It was hard to imagine what the little man with the potbelly had on his mind. Was he going to take us all to jail? It didn't seem so, and also it was practically impossible. We didn't mind standing in the middle of our village square, but not even all those armed men would have been enough to take us to the city and lock us up.

We recognized these men in black shirts for

other reasons. To give themselves courage they had to come during the night. Most of them smelled of wine, yet they hadn't the guts to look you in the eye. They were poor people too. But they formed a special class of poor people—without land, without a trade or with many trades (which is the same thing), rebels against all hard work. Too weak and cowardly to stand up to the rich and the authorities, they preferred to serve them so they could rob and oppress the others—the peasants, tenants and small landowners. They were humble and obsequious when you met them on the street during the day. When they formed in groups during the night, they were wicked and treacherous. They have always been in the service of whoever gives the orders, and they always will be. But now they had their own army with its own uniform and its own guns. These were the so-called Fascists.

But there was another reason for their strength. Any one of us could beat up three of them. But at this moment what did we have in common with one another, all of us who had been born in Fontamara, as we had? Nothing—except that we were at the same place at the same time! Beyond this, everyone thought of his own affairs. Everyone was trying to think of his own way to get out of the formation of armed men and to leave the others in. Everyone was the head of a family and was thinking of his family. Maybe Berardo was thinking of something else, but he had no land and no wife.

Meanwhile it had got late.

"Well," said Berardo, "let's get going!"

The little man with the belly was impressed with his tone of voice and said:

"Now let's start the examination."

"Examination? What examination? Are we in school?"

A gap about a yard wide was made in the formation, with the potbellied man on one side and Filippo on the other, just like the shepherds in the stalls when they milk the sheep.

This is how the examination began.

The first person called was Teofilo the sacristan.

"What are you for?" the man with the three-colored badge briskly asked him. Teofilo didn't know what to make of the question.

"What are you for?" repeated the irritated representative of the authorities.

Teofilo turned his amazed countenance to us as if to ask for suggestions. But each one of us knew as much as he did. And since the poor man continued to give signs of not knowing what to answer, the bellied one turned to Filippo il Bello, who had a large register in his hands, and commanded him:

"Write next to his name, *recusant*."

Teofilo went away in great consternation. The second to be called was Anacleto the tailor.

"What are you for?" the man with the belly asked him.

Anacleto, who had had time to think about it, answered:

"I'm for the Madonna."

"Which Madonna?" Filippo asked him.

Anacleto thought about it a while, seemed to hesitate, then he said:

"The one of Loreto."

"Write *recusant*," ordered the little man to Filippo with disgust in his voice.

Anacleto didn't want to go. He said he was willing to mention the Madonna of Pompeii rather than the one of Loreto, but he was rudely shoved aside. The third to be called was old Braciola. He had his answer ready and cried:

"Long live San Rocco!"

But that answer didn't satisfy the little man either. He ordered the roadman:

"Write *recusant*."

The fourth to be called up was Cipolla.

"What are you for?" he was asked.

"Excuse me, what does that mean?" he was bold enough to ask.

"Answer sincerely what you think," the little man said. "What are you for?"

"I'm for bread and wine," was the prompt and sincere answer of Cipolla. He was also registered as a recusant. Every one of us awaited his turn and no one could imagine what the representative of the authorities wanted us to answer to this strange question about what we were for.

We were mainly concerned with what we would have to pay if we gave the wrong answer. No one of us knew what a recusant was, but, likely as not, it meant "obliged to pay." In other words, it was just another excuse to take money away from us. For my part, I tried to get close to Baldissera for some advice on my answer, since he knew more than any of us about ceremonies. But he looked at me with a smile of compassion, like someone who knows a lot of things and intends to use them only to his own advantage.

"What are you for?" the little man of the law asked Baldissera.

The old shoemaker took off his cap and cried:

"Long live Queen Margaret!"

The effect wasn't at all what Baldissera expected. The soldiers all burst out laughing, and the little man informed him:

"She's dead. Queen Margaret is dead."

"She's dead?" asked Baldissera in great pain. "Impossible!"

"Write *constitutionalist,*" he said to Filippo il Bello with a disparaging smile.

Baldissera had gone off, shaking his head at this train of inexplicable events. He was followed by Antonio La Zappa, who cried (on Berardo's instructions):

"Down with the thieves!"

This provoked a general protest among the men in black, who took it as a personal insult.

"Write *anarchist,*" said the fat man to Filippo il Bello.

La Zappa went off laughing, and it was Spaventa's turn.

"Down with the vagabonds!" cried Spaventa, causing many murmurs in the ranks of the examiners. And he too was registered as an anarchist.

"What are you for?" asked the bellied one of Della Croce.

But he was a pupil of Berardo also and was never for things but against them. So he answered:

"Down with the taxes!"

This time, be it said truthfully, the men in black and their leader didn't protest.

But Della Croce was put down as an anarchist, because, as the little man stated, certain things just aren't said.

Raffaele Scarpone made a bigger impression, yelling almost in the face of the man of the law:

"Down with the man who pays you!"

The man was horrified, as if Raffaele had uttered the most horrible blasphemy, and wanted to arrest him, but Raffaele had taken care to speak only after he had got out of the square, and in two seconds he was behind the church and nobody saw him again.

With Losurdo the procession of prudent persons began again:

"Long live everybody!" he answered laughing.

It was hard to imagine a more prudent answer, but it was not appreciated.

"Write *liberal*," said the little man to Filippo il Bello.

"Long live the government!" yelled Uliva with the best possible good humor.

"Which government?" Filippo il Bello asked out of curiosity. Uliva had never heard that there were different governments, but his training led him to answer:

"The legitimate government."

"Write *traitor*," said potbelly to Filippo.

Pilato wanted to try something, and since it was his turn, he said:

"Long live the government!"

"Which government?" asked Filippo, alarmed.

"The illegitimate government."

"Write *rascal*," said the fat man.

In other words, none of us had been able to come out with the right answer. As the number of wrong answers mounted up, the choice of answers for those who remained got smaller and smaller. But what we had not found out yet was whether we had to pay if we gave the wrong answer, and how much. Only Berardo didn't seem worried about this and amused himself by suggesting impudent answers to the boys in his group, all of which involved being against and not for something.

"Down with the bank!" yelled Venerdì Santo.

"What bank?" asked Filippo.

"There's just one bank, and it gives money to the Trader!" answered the well-informed Venerdì.

"Write *communist*," said the little man to Filippo.

Gasparone was also put down as a communist when at the question as to what he was for he answered:

"Down with Torlonia!"

Palummo was put down as a socialist for having very courteously answered:

"Long live the poor!"

Just then, Maria Rosa, Berardo's mother, appeared from the other side of the square. We had seen her come down from the street and go into Maria Grazia's house, which is at the beginning of the path leading up from the church.

"Berardo! Where's Berardo?" the old woman was yelling. "Do you know what these bastards have done in our houses? Do you know what they've done to the women? And our men? Where are our men? Where's Berardo?"

Berardo understood at once, at least he thought he did. In one leap he was next to Filippo il Bello, who was livid with fear. He grabbed him by the collar, spat in his face and asked:

"Where's Elvira? What have you done with Elvira?"

Old Maria Rosa was at the church door and on her knees. She began to cry:

"Mary, defend us! Mary, intervene! Because our

men aren't good for anything."

The old woman hadn't finished her invocation when a stroke of the bell attracted everyone's attention to the church tower.

By the side of the great bell we discovered a strange apparition: the sight of a tall, thin young woman whose face was as white as snow and whose hands were folded on her breast. For an instant none of us breathed. Then the vision disappeared.

"The Madonna! The Madonna!" howled Filippo il Bello in terror.

"The Madonna! The Madonna!" yelled the other men in black, seized by the same fear.

The formation broke up and the soldiers ran in panic to their trucks, which they had left at the entrance to the village. The little man of the law ran with them.

We heard the noise of the motors from far off. Then we saw the trucks going back down the hill in a rush, with their lights on. There were so many we couldn't count them.

At the foot of the hill, at the last curve just before the national highway, we saw the procession of trucks suddenly stop. They stopped for half an hour.

"Why did they stop? Are they coming back?" I asked Berardo.

"Maybe Scarpone knows why they stopped," he told me, laughing.

(The next day, we found that the trucks had

stopped at the bottom of the hill because a tree trunk had been laid across the road. The first truck couldn't avoid it and several had been injured, among them the little man with the three-colored badge.)

It was late by the time the trucks had gone.

"Should we go to bed, or should we wait a little longer and start for the fields?" I asked Berardo.

"First of all, we should find out who's in the church tower!" Berardo answered me.

In fact, Berardo believed in the Devil, but not in Mary. The appearance of the Devil would have convinced him, but not the appearance of the Virgin. We went up to the church tower, and to our surprise we found my wife and Elvira. The girl hadn't yet recovered consciousness.

What could we do? We couldn't wait for dawn up there, but it wasn't easy to bring her down that ladder in the dark. I was in front and held her feet, and in back Berardo held her shoulders.

She was no better when she reached the square. She couldn't answer any questions and couldn't stay on her feet. I don't deny that it was I who proposed to Berardo:

"Look, if you've carried her this far, you might as well take her the rest of the way."

He picked her up in his arms, and holding her as easily as a shepherd holds a lamb, he disappeared into the darkness toward her house.

6.

The following morning Maria Rosa came to see me.

"Have you seen my son?" she asked me. "Did he sleep at your house? I haven't slept a wink waiting for him."

I was very much surprised at what she said, but I didn't tell Berardo's mother what I was thinking.

The poor woman went slowly up the street, and I saw her at Scarpone's door, asking him if he had seen Berardo. Later, when I was packing the donkey, Maria Rosa came by again and said, hoping to excuse her son:

"You know, Berardo isn't bad, but my poor son was born unlucky. What hard luck he was born to, my poor son."

But as I was going out to the fields, guiding the donkey past the church tower, I ran into Berardo himself.

"I went to your place," he said to me without looking me in the face (and his voice sounded very strange). "I had something to say to you."

"Your mother is looking all over for you," I answered with emotion in my voice, driving the donkey to make him go faster.

But Berardo didn't make anything of it and walked along with me, guessing from the tone of my voice that I knew everything.

"Don't get mad!" he said to me. "What happened had to happen."

"It seems to me," I said to him, interrupting, "that you are tempting fate."

"It's not true," he protested vigorously, taking me by the arm with a viselike grip. "You know it's not true! You know my life hasn't been easy! You know I haven't let things slide!"

And after a brief pause, he added firmly but quietly, almost whispering:

"And now I'm less resigned than ever."

"What do you think you're going to do?" I asked him.

"I'm going to get married," he said. "But first of all I have to get settled. That's important. I have to get some land. I think you'll agree to that."

"Well, it's not easy to get land these days," I observed. "You should know this. You've already tried twice and you haven't succeeded."

"I'll try again!" he said with energy and unusual optimism. "I'll try again, and this time, you'll see, I'll succeed. Now it's not only me. It's not only my life; I feel ten times as strong. You'll see."

"Strength has nothing to do with it," I wanted to say to him. "It doesn't depend on you, or on your need. It's not easy to get land at Fontamara. . . ." But when I looked in his face that morning as I never had before, I suddenly felt great compassion for him. It was as if I had seen his entire future all at once, and I was so moved that I tried to conceal my inexplicable disturbance.

"God bless you, Berardo," I stammered. "I can say nothing else. May God help you!"

But he must have known how I felt, because he was quite moved himself. He took leave of me hurriedly and went back for his hoe.

I was to think of Berardo all that day, and of his urgent need to find land. For otherwise his pride would not permit him to marry Elvira, though by now he was obliged to do so. To understand this way of thinking, you must consider the condition of the landless peasant in our part of the world in recent years. At Fontamara and neighboring villages, most of the farmers are small landowners or tenants or both together. Very few have no land at all. The peasant with no land is despised by everyone. Because the price of land is low, the farm hand who has none is considered lazy and stupid. At one time this was almost always a true judgment, but later the conditions changed. Where we lived there weren't any more small landowners who enlarged their holding, nor were there any farm hands who bought land. On the contrary, it even happened that the small landowner fell into the peasant class. But even though times had changed, the old way of thinking had remained, and the peasant without land was still held in contempt.

It is true that in many ways Berardo was an exceptional peasant, and nobody claimed to despise him. For his poverty was the result, not of laziness or of ignorance, but of misfortune. He himself, however, who usually acted so proud, felt wretched and unworthy at the thought of marrying a girl like Elvira when he hadn't any land.

All that day, as I was mowing hay in one of don Carlo Magna's meadows, I thought of the sad and dangerous condition Elvira was in, and I came to the conclusion that the only way out would be to find Berardo five or six months of some heavy work in the city—the kind of work that the city people refuse to do, the kind that is better paid than the work in the fields. Perhaps he could buy something when he got back with what he had saved. But where could one go for good advice without running the risk of new frauds? Not to the priest, not to the landowner, not to the lawyer. Recent events had very much discouraged us.

Not even Baldissera was any good. He was the most disturbed of all of us at all these strange things that were happening. The old ceremonious world he had believed in was dead, and in its place there occurred crazy and inexplicable things.

Soldiers had come to Fontamara and raped several women. This was an outrage, nevertheless an understandable one. But that it had been done in the name of the law and in the presence of the chief of police was not understandable at all.

At Fucino the rent of the small tenants had been raised and that of the large tenants lowered, and this was more or less natural. But the proposal had come from the representatives of the small tenants, and this was completely unnatural.

The so-called Fascists had several times beaten, wounded and even killed people who had done nothing but annoy the Trader, and even this might seem natural. But the thugs and assassins had been rewarded by the authorities, and this was entirely inexplicable. In short, it could be said that everything that had happened to us recently was not new and had ample precedents in the past. But the way everything happened was absurd, and we could find no explanation at all for this.

The little grain that was to go to Fontamara after the harvest had been reserved by the Trader since the end of May, when it was still green, at a hundred and twenty lire per quintal. The Trader's offer had seemed to us to be an opportunity that should be taken up. It was strange that the usually prudent Trader should buy grain in May, when no one knows what the market will be. But we had needed money, and without a second thought we had all sold our grain when it was still green. And so had the farmers of nearby villages.

During the harvest the mystery was revealed to us. The government had made a law in favor of home-grown grain, and its price rose at once from a hundred and twenty to a hundred and seventy lire per quintal. Evidently the Trader had known about the law since the month of May. With no effort whatsoever, he made fifty lire on every quintal of grain before it was even harvested. In this way the entire profit from the cultivation of our grain had gone to the Trader. All the profit of the plowing, the weeding, the harvesting, the threshing—all the profit of a year's work, of sweat, pain and suffering, had gone to that foreigner, who had never had anything to do with the land. The peasants plowed, leveled the ground, hoed, harvested and threshed, and when everything was finished, a foreigner came along and took all the profit.

Who could protest? You couldn't even protest, because everything was legal. Only the protest itself would have been illegal.

For a long time robbing the peasants had been legal. When the old laws hadn't been enough, new ones had been made.

"I'm not going to stay here," Berardo kept telling me anxiously. "I've got to get away. But where?"

Everyone saw how Berardo suffered. He was no longer the man he had once been. He didn't joke or laugh and he avoided company. Now we could see that there was a thorn in his side and that his heart was bleeding.

"Only don Circostanza can help you," I had to tell him. "He has so many connections."

Berardo, Scarpone and I had a bit of business with don Circostanza, for we had replanted in an old vineyard of his behind the cemetery some vines that had been half uprooted last year by a flood. One Sunday morning we went to his house to be paid and to give Berardo a chance to ask him for some work in the city.

"Only the People's Friend can help you," I said to Berardo.

Don Circostanza shook our hands and greeted us with great cordiality.

"How many days' pay do I owe you?" he asked us.

Berardo had fifteen days, Raffaele and I had twelve; it oughtn't to have been difficult for an educated person like don Circostanza. But suddenly the People's Friend put on a long face. He was silent for several minutes. He looked out the window and peeped through the keyhole to see if anyone was listening. Then he came up to us and said in a low voice:

"It's terrible. You can't imagine how the government persecutes us. Every day the government invents a new law against us. We aren't even free to use our own money."

These words impressed us. Was the government persecuting even the gentlemen?

"Sir, you have only to say the word," answered Berardo in a tone of voice he hadn't used for quite a while, "and all the peasants will revolt."

"That doesn't have anything to do with it," said don Circostanza. "It's a more refined type of outrage. Here are the three envelopes I had prepared for you, one for each of you, with the pay we agreed on."

There were three envelopes on the table.

"I had everything ready," he continued, "just as

we agreed. I hadn't taken out a single centesimo.
Do you believe me?"

Why shouldn't we have believed him?

Then we shook hands once more with great cordiality.

"But now," he continued, "I have received the
new work contract for agricultural labor in the
province. It was a terrible blow to me. Read it with
your own eyes."

I mistrustfully took a newspaper don Circostanza
gave me, and at his insistence, read some passages
underlined in red. According to what was written,
the prevailing wage for agricultural workers was
reduced by forty per cent for men from nineteen
to sixty. That is, for us.

"Isn't it terrible?" he said. "Keep on reading.
It's not finished yet."

I read that work on improvements; new plantings or replantings of vines, olive and fruit trees;
constructions of manure pots; emptying, cleaning
or digging of ditches; and the opening of roads
had the character of extraordinary undertakings intended to relieve unemployment and, as such, must
be paid for with wages inferior by twenty-five per
cent to the established ones.

"Isn't it insupportable?" continued the lawyer.
"What has the law to do with the farmer and the
landowner? What will happen to our liberty?"

The swindle was obvious. It was a new scheme
to rob us in the name of the law. Don Circostanza

had always been the master of such affairs. Among
other things, he had had the shrewdness to buy up
three unpayable notes at a local bank at a fourth
or a third of their value and had the farmers pay
for them in days of work, so that the peasants
worked without wages and he took it out in misery.
Therefore we had had a little examination of conscience before we had gone into his office. We had
asked ourselves:

"Does any of us have a note outstanding with
him? Some long-forgotten note?"

No one had. But this time the swindle was different.

"Here are the three envelopes," observed Berardo. "We'll take them and everything will be settled."

And Berardo was about to take his envelope. But
don Circostanza, who was waiting for this, prevented him from doing so.

"What?" he yelled in a different tone of voice
from that he had just used. "Are such things to
happen in my house?"

I intervened immediately to prevent Berardo
from compromising himself.

"What's wrong with that?" I asked. "We have
worked so many days for a given wage. It isn't
hard to figure out what we should get. We can be
friends as before."

"And the law!" he yelled at me. "What will happen to the law? Do you know what penalties you

risk if you break a law like that? You don't know. You are ignorant. But I know. I'm not going to jail for your sakes. I'm very sorry, but I can't go to jail for your sakes. The law's the law. You have to respect it."

"Moses' law says, 'Thou shalt not steal,' " I added.

"Moses' law is for the Heavenly Court," don Circostanza replied to me. "Here the government rules. What's more, I'm not the one who has to enforce the law. If you won't obey peacefully, I'll have to call the police."

This last remark produced a strange effect, and don Circostanza himself seemed to regret that he had said it. It was like the blow of a whip in the face to Berardo. He suddenly got up, but I went up to him and made him sit down. There was an embarrassing silence.

"I hope there's no misunderstanding," the lawyer stammered. "These are hard times for me also."

This was pretty much the truth. On the wall of his office there was a large photograph of his son, who had died in the war, and near that one of his wife, who was in an insane asylum. When you looked at don Circostanza, you realized that he was no longer the lucky and cheerful man he had once been. But that was no reason for our being disturbed. We were a lot worse off than he.

"When the shepherd is ill, the whole flock is in

trouble," he added, almost as if to answer our thoughts.

Berardo was like a man in chains who frets and fusses but can't free himself from his bonds and doesn't even want to. He seemed very discouraged and humiliated and didn't even look Scarpone in the face.

"How much?" asked Berardo through his teeth.

Don Circostanza was very much surprised at Berardo's unusual humility and had the bad taste to congratulate him.

"If you had always shown the same good sense you show now," he said to him, "not to reproach you, but you would be a lot better off."

He went to his desk, picked up Berardo's envelope and took the money out of it. He took a piece of paper and a pencil and began to stutter out the figures:

"According to the law," he said, "we must first of all take off forty per cent. From what's left, according to the law, we take twenty-five per cent as a contribution to unemployment. Berardo gets thirty-eight lire. My dear Berardo, I'm very sorry, but it's the government's fault."

Fifteen days of heavy work for a miserable thirty-eight lire!

Then don Circostanza took my envelope and took out the money. He began scribbling his figures on it.

"According to the law, we begin by taking out

forty per cent. Then we take out twenty-five per cent as a contribution to unemployment. This leaves thirty-four lire."

He did the same thing on Scarpone's envelope.

Thirty-four lire for twelve days of hard labor! These ridiculous wages seemed so unrelated to our work that it looked like witchery to us. I asked myself whether it was worth the trouble to work the land only to be tricked like that. Berardo said nothing, but certainly he had something on his mind. Scarpone was looking at him as if he didn't believe his eyes. His astonishment at Berardo's behavior didn't allow him time to be angry at don Circostanza.

As a generous gesture to prove there were no hard feelings, don Circostanza called the maid and offered us a glass of wine.

I'm afraid we drank it. When we were leaving, I signaled Berardo to remain.

"I would like to have a word with you," said Berardo to the lawyer as he took us to the door. "I need some advice."

I promised that we would wait for him on the road, and I kept Scarpone with me. He thought —and hoped—that Berardo would finally give don Circostanza a piece of his mind and wanted to stay behind to help him.

"Berardo's no kid," I said to Scarpone in a reproachful voice. "It's time he ran his own affairs."

"You people who have minded your own busi-

ness haven't done so well!" he answered contemptu-
ously.

On the road we found Baldovino Sciarappa, who
was scolding his wife loudly, blaming her entirely
for the ruin of their household. The poor woman
was begging him to be quiet and to postpone the
discussions, reproaches and beatings until they
were at home, but this only made the husband more
angry.

Baldovino rented a small piece of land from don
Carlo Magna, and he had just paid his rent. But
to his great surprise, donna Clorinda had found
the payment insufficient because last year his wife
had brought two dozen eggs along with the rent as
a present, and on the basis of the law fixed by custom, donna Clorinda now demanded the two dozen
eggs every year along with the rent. Actually, the
unhappy idea of bringing the eggs had been Baldovino's, but his wife had brought them. She had not
explained that this was only a present. Therefore
Baldovino claimed that it was all his wife's fault.
As a result, for that year, for the next year and
for all the rest of Baldovino's life, and all the rest
of his son's life, donna Clorinda would claim those
two dozen eggs on the grounds that under the law
of custom they were due.

At least one thing was clear: new laws were coming out every day in favor of the landowners. But
only the old laws that were in favor of the peasants
were being abolished. The ones that were unfavor-

able remained. And what was worse, donna Clorinda, following the old custom of the landowners, had a large ring in her kitchen to measure the size of the eggs that her tenants brought her as presents. And she systematically refused all those that were small enough to go through the ring. Now this ring dated back to a time when, for some reason or other, the hens had laid bigger eggs. She kept on refusing more and more eggs and asking for bigger ones. Was it the peasants' fault that the hens weren't laying bigger eggs? And, anyway, the eggs were presents.

Berardo came to us with a letter in his hand.

"He promised to help me," he said. "Don Circostanza wrote a letter for me to a friend of his in Rome."

"So you still believe in the promise of the People's Friend," said Scarpone with a wry smile.

"No," answered Berardo, "but I think don Circostanza would get me a job, just to get rid of me."

In spite of everything, Berardo was all too prone to fool himself. Once more he was laughing and joking. That evening he came back to Marietta's place after a long absence. Unfortunately he arrived there when Americo was talking about Elvira. Certainly he wasn't saying anything offensive, but in any event, he was talking about her. Berardo politely asked him to step outside a moment, as if he had just remembered something trivial. He brought him back very shortly thereafter, bleeding from his mouth and one ear, and asked Marietta to wash him carefully with fresh water and vinegar.

About that time Teofilo the sacristan was making a collection so that don Abbacchio could come to Fontamara and say a Mass for the people. He managed to collect about ten lire, but don Abbacchio answered that the price of the Mass had gone up, and that he couldn't come unless there were at least ten lire more. With great effort ten more lire were collected, penny by penny, and one morning don Abbacchio came to say Mass.

To attract the men as well, he announced that during the sermon he would tell the story of San Giuseppe da Copertino. As a matter of fact, the church was full. Even Berardo had come when he heard what the sermon was to be about. The church was in very poor condition, what with the bullet holes made by the men in black when they shot at the windows. The only really beautiful thing was the painting of the Eucharist on the altar. Jesus had a little piece of white bread in his hand and was saying:

"This is My body. The white bread is My body. The white bread is the Son of God. The white bread is truth and life."

Jesus didn't mean the corn bread that the peasants ate, nor the insipid substitute bread the priests use as a host. Jesus had a real piece of white bread in his hand and was saying:

"This bread here [the white bread] *is My body."*

That is, the body of the Son of God. That is God, truth and life. And He meant: whoever has white bread has Me, has God. He who doesn't have white bread, he who has only corn bread, is not in a state of grace, doesn't know the truth, and has no life. Like the pigs or the donkeys or the goats, he feeds on impurities. If you have no white bread, if you have only corn bread, it is as if Christ had never been, as if there had never been a Redemption, as if Christ were yet to come. How could we not think of our grain, which had been cultivated with such great labor all year, and which had been bought up by the bank in the month of May when it was still green and resold at a great profit. We had raised it with the sweat of our brow, but we weren't to eat it. It was to go to town; everyone would eat it, even the gentlemen's cats and dogs. But we weren't to eat it. We were to eat corn bread. But Christ, saying from the altar, "This is My body," didn't have a piece of corn bread, but a piece of fancy white bread.

And the invocation of the paternoster—"Give us this day our daily bread"—certainly didn't mean corn bread, but white bread. And the bread in the sacramental song—"O living bread of Heaven"— is surely not corn bread, but white bread.

When don Abbacchio came to the gospel lesson,

he turned to us and announced a little sermon on
the life of San Giuseppe da Copertino. We knew
his story, but we always liked to hear it again. This
saint was a peasant and joined a monastery. He
never was able to learn Latin. When the other broth-
ers recited the psalms, he honored the Virgin wherever he was, even in Church, by doing somersaults.
Holy Mary must have been delighted at this innocent spectacle, and to reward and encourage him
she gave him the gift of levitation. From that moment on, he somersaulted to the ceiling with no
trouble at all. San Giuseppe da Copertino died at
an advanced age after a life of dire privations.
They say that when he appeared before the Divine
Throne, God, who had heard so much about him
from the Virgin, already liked him. He embraced
him and said:

"Anything you want you can have. Don't be
ashamed to ask for anything you want."

The poor saint was very much disturbed at this
offer.

"Can I ask for anything?" he inquired timidly.

"Anything at all," answered the Eternal Father,
encouraging him. "I run things up here in Heaven.
Up here I can do anything I feel like. I really like
you, and anything you want, you can have."

But San Giuseppe da Copertino didn't dare make
his request. He was afraid that his immodest de-
sires would make God angry. Only after God had

insisted and given His word of honor that He wouldn't be angry, the saint asked for what he wanted.

"Lord, I want a nice big piece of white bread."

God kept His word and did not get angry, but embraced the holy peasant and wept with him for a long time. Then in a thunderous voice He called twelve angels and ordered that every day from morning to night throughout all the ages they furnish him with the best white bread baked in Paradise.

This is the real story of San Giuseppe da Copertino, which is told from father to son in our village. Nobody can guarantee that that's exactly how it happened. But it was a story we liked very much at Fontamara, and we never got tired of hearing it repeated.

Don Abbacchio used it only as a pretext, then he went on to scold us for our bad behavior, and he threatened us with the wrath of God if things didn't improve. We listened without saying anything, the way you usually do at such things, until don Abbacchio had the unfortunate idea of scolding us for not having paid our taxes!

"Pay! There's always something to pay!" interrupted Berardo Viola in a loud voice, and he went out of the church. One by one all the men followed him out, leaving only the women and children inside.

Don Abbacchio realized something was wrong,

finished the Mass in a hurry, took off his chasuble and surplice and came out of the sacristy in a bad mood.

He was not really a wicked man, but lazy, cowardly and not to be trusted with serious matters. He certainly wasn't the sort of shepherd who would risk his life to defend his sheep from the wolves, but he was well enough informed in his religion to explain to us how from the moment that God created the wolves he gave them the right to devour a sheep from time to time. We went to him for the sacraments. But we knew from experience that we could get no help or advice that would deliver us from the wickedness of the rich and powerful. As they say, pay attention to what the priest says, not to what he does. We couldn't trust even him.

When he came out of the sacristy, he met Baldissera, who was leaning against the wall and slowly (very slowly so that no one could see what he was doing) was rubbing his back against it to scrape off the lice.

"How are you?" asked the priest, just to start a conversation.

"I'm fine!" answered the general with a bow.

But he got various less complimentary answers from the men who were waiting for the women in the square.

"You seem to forget that it was God who established that you are to earn your bread with the sweat of your brow," the priest called out.

The unfortunate don Abbacchio didn't know that this was a sore subject. Five or six men answered. Then Berardo drowned out the rest.

"If only the world were run by that rule," said Berardo.

"Why? Don't you find that it is so?" asked the priest.

"If only I did earn my daily bread with the sweat of my brow. Actually I earn bread for people who don't work."

"You can be useful to society without hoeing the earth," the priest said.

"How does it go?" continued Berardo, getting a little hot under the collar. "It says, 'You shall earn your daily bread.' It doesn't say it the way it really happens. You shall earn spaghetti, coffee and liquor for the Trader."

"My job is religion, not politics," interrupted the priest, who was very angry. He started to go away.

But Berardo took him by the arm and held him, amid the general laughter.

"How does it go?" asked Berardo again. "It says, 'With the sweat of your brow.' It doesn't say it the way it really happens—with your blood, with the marrow of your bones, with your life!"

"If you had been a monk, you would have been a great preacher," don Abbacchio answered Berardo in all seriousness.

And with that he turned the laughter in his favor and saved himself. When he had arrived, he had given us two fingers when he shook hands. When he left, he gave us only one.

"In the good years a priest is a good thing," concluded Michele Zompa. "He says Mass, the triduum and the novenas. He baptizes, gives communion and extreme unction, preaches funeral sermons, and if there's enough money all is well, like cheese on macaroni. But when there's a famine, what can a poor priest do for us? When there is a famine, the peasants have only one resort, to quarrel among themselves."

At Fontamara no two families were at peace with each other. The most violent fights arose on the smallest of pretexts. They began during the day among the women and children and started up again in the evening when the men got back. At one time it was over some borrowed yeast that hadn't been paid back; at another it was about a brick, or a barrel, or a piece of iron, or some wood, or a hen, or some straw. When people are miserable, they find dozens of excuses to quarrel every day. But for us the greatest cause of all was always the water of the stream.

The roadmen had finally finished digging the new stream bed, and on the day of the division of the water all the peasants of Fontamara interested in the irrigation were there, together with Baldissera and the usual loafers.

At the point where the water was to be divided, two gates had been built to lead off some of the water to the Trader and leave some in the stream —that is, the mysterious three quarters and three quarters.

The gentlemen showed a bad conscience from the first. In fact, there were about a hundred policemen from the city, who lined up on the bank. A squad of them came to us and with kicks and shoves pushed us away from the stream toward the vineyards. We let them do it because we had never seen so many policemen before.

"It's war!" said Baldissera, quite disturbed. "It's real war!"

"It's war against the peasants!" added Michele. "There are too many of us!"

Scarpone was desperately looking for Berardo.

"Something ought to be done about it," he said. "Where is Berardo? Haven't any of you seen Berardo?"

Berardo's absence was much more demoralizing than all those policemen.

Scarpone took me aside. He was almost in tears.

"You know where Berardo is," he said. "Tell me where he is and I'll send for him right away. He couldn't be away on a day like this! Not him!"

I didn't tell him the truth.

"I don't know," I answered. "I really don't know. Maybe he'll come later."

A little later two groups of soldiers arrived, detachments from the troops that had come to Fontamara the night of the examination. And after them came the High Society: the Trader, the notary, don Circostanza, the famous little man with the three-colored badge, don Abbacchio, Cavaliere Pelino, some other gentlemen we didn't know and, behind them all, Filippo il Bello and Innocenzo La Legge.

Don Circostanza came up and shook hands with all of us, telling us to trust him for our own good. He would do all he could for us, but he admitted that our cause was nearly hopeless. We had compromised it with our bad behavior.

"Where is Berardo?" he asked. "I warn you. Keep him away!"

It was established that we were to name a commission of older men. Pilato, Losurdo and I were called. The other peasants were allowed to assemble on the road behind a cordon of policemen.

All these so different spectators, gathered in such a wide space and concentrating their gaze on the same point, reminded you of an open-air circus. Or if you observed all of Fontamara and the policemen, it might look to you like the scene of some horrible murder. The body would be lying where the gates were. The whole scene was like the erection of a new cross in the country, a new Calvary.

"Where's Berardo?" asked Filippo il Bello in a whisper.

"He's coming!" I answered him, and he turned pale.

The notary came up and read the agreement be-

tween the population of Fontamara and the Trader
for the division of the water.

"The agreement is clear as day," he said. "Three
quarters of the water is to go into the new bed dug
by the town and the rest will run in the old stream."

"No! No!" protested Pilato. "The agreement
says three quarters and three quarters. Nothing
more. Therefore it's half and half. Three quarters
to the Trader and three quarters to us. The same
for each."

"Not at all!" yelled Losurdo. "The agreement
isn't like that. The agreement says that we must
have three quarters of the water, and the rest, if
there's any left, goes to the Trader. But there might
not be any left. Even then it's wrong!"

"Three quarters and three quarters is nonsense!"
I said, losing my patience. "I never heard of such
a thing! The truth is that the water belongs to Fontamara and should stay that way!"

Our villagers, surrounded on the road by policemen, realized from our gestures that the water
was to be divided to our disadvantage and began
to complain. Scarpone, especially, yelled like a
demon, aided by his usual group of brainless
youngsters.

"Since the people of Fontamara insist on a pro-
vocative attitude, and the members of the commission of older men aren't in agreement among themselves," said the Trader, "in my capacity as head
of the town, I nominate the Cavaliere Pelino and

don Circostanza to be representatives of Fontamara. Any objections?" he asked the gentlemen around him.

"The ruling is legal!" declared don Circostanza in our name.

"Most definitely legal!" said the rest of them.

"Let's get going!" ordered the Trader, who was in a bad mood. "I haven't any time to waste!"

He had an incredible nerve. He was the defendant, prosecutor, judge and jury, all in one.

Six policemen threw themselves on us and shoved us over to where the rest of the villagers were. Don Circostanza cried to us:

"Trust me! Keep calm!"

From behind the policemen we could follow only a little of what went on at the stream. To tell the truth, I wasn't too disappointed, because I no longer had any responsibility in the eyes of the other peasants.

We vaguely saw the notary, then an architect, then four roadmen with their shovels come up to the stream.

Cavaliere Pelino and don Circostanza were seen at various times also discussing matters with the architect.

But the rise in the road, together with the great crowd of policemen and authorities around the two specialists who were to help regulate the division of the water, prevented us from seeing how the damned "three quarters and three quarters" was to be interpreted. About a hundred yards further on, however, where the old bed of the stream made a bend between Barletta's and Papasisto's plots, we could distinctly see how much of our water was to be taken away and how much was to remain. Therefore we were looking down there. We were trying to guess what the authorities and our representatives were deciding only a few paces from us.

Scarpone was the first to observe that the water level was going down. Though none of us thought that the quantity of water would remain as before, we all began cursing the Trader and the High Society when we saw the level going down. The level of our water went to half of what it was, but didn't stop there.

"Thieves! Thieves! Thieves!" we shouted.

The Quaterna and Recchiuta girls, Cannarozzo's daughter, Giuditta, the Limona girl, Marietta and some other women knelt down on the ground and began screaming the most horrible curses that they could think of, shaking their fists at the sky:

"May they lose as much blood as they have taken water from us!"

"May they weep as many tears as they have taken water from us!"

"May toads grow in their stomachs!"

"May water snakes grow in their guts!"

"May none of them see their wives or children again!"

The policemen nearest to us distinctly heard all

these curses and were frightened. They begged the
women:

"That's enough! Stop!"

But this only excited the women more.

"May they die in the desert!"

"May they be eternally damned!"

"Jesus, Joseph, Saint Anne and Saint Mary,
grant this prayer to my soul!"

Meanwhile the level of our water continued to
go down in the part of the stream we could observe.
Finally the stones and the little water plants began
to emerge from the bottom of the stream.

"Consummatum est!" we heard don Abbacchio
say.

"They've taken every drop of the water!" we
began to scream. Scarpone and Venerdì Santo, sup-
ported by some other youngsters, charged the group
of policemen that held us on the road. They defended themselves, using their rifles as clubs, strik-
ing like madmen, shouting:

"Get back! Get back!"

After a great deal of trouble, don Circostanza's
voice emerged from the confusion.

"Take it easy!" he yelled. "I'm here to defend
your interests! Let me handle it! Don't do anything
stupid! Don't compromise yourselves!"

Don Circostanza came up to us on the shoulder
of the road and made one of his usual speeches. I'm
afraid we listened to him.

"Don't you trust me? That's why your affairs are

so badly off. Do you think all this screaming and shouting is going to do any good?"

Then he turned to the Trader and said:

"These people are quite rightly disturbed. We must reach some compromise. The people of Fontamara are good people and should be respected. The town has already spent the money to dig a new ditch for the two gates. What has been done has been done. It is a saying of Christ, *Quod factum est, factum est.*"

"Are you trying to do my work?" interrupted don Abbacchio, laughing, and all the High Society laughed with him.

"We could set up a time after which all the water could go back to Fontamara," proposed don Circostanza. "That should reassure them. Their loss is legal? Yes, but not eternal. Someone propose something!"

"Fifty years!" proposed the Trader.

A scream of indignation greeted this shameless proposal, and some people yelled who hadn't even heard it.

"Why don't you cut all our throats? We'd rather spend the rest of our lives in jail! Thief! Thief!" we yelled at the top of our voices.

Don Circostanza was able to re-establish silence, and having turned to the Trader, said:

"Fifty years is too long! We'll have to set a shorter time."

"Forty years," proposed don Abbacchio.

"Thirty-five years," proposed Cavaliere Pelino.

"Twenty-five years," proposed the notary.

It was like a circus. Every proposal was answered with our refusal. And, as usual, people yelled who hadn't heard the proposals. But what good was it to have heard them? Every word and gesture from these gentlemen reeked of trickery. Finally the little man with the three-colored badge entered into action, ordering the policemen to shove us back still farther. It wasn't pleasant for them, but the shoves and blows and kicks we exchanged made us lose sight of what was happening at the gates.

At one point we saw the notary with a piece of paper in his hand.

"Paper!" yelled Scarpone with the anger of someone who finally sees the swindle with his own eyes.

Baldissera couldn't see that far. "Is there paper already?" he asked anxiously. "Well, the swindle is complete!"

We saw the gentlemen gather around the paper for a few minutes, and saw them finally shake hands and exchange bows all around. But we couldn't hear their voices.

(Afterwards they told us the loss of the water was for ten lustra, and it seemed that the proposal had been advanced in our favor by don Circostanza, but none of us knew how many months or how many years ten lustra were.)

7.

There were many discussions at Fontamara as to how long ten lustra were. Baldissera claimed that it was ten centuries.

"Couldn't it be ten months?" Marietta tried to suggest. But nobody agreed with her.

In any case, the ten lustra meant hunger for Fontamara. At the foot of the hill the fields and gardens abandoned by the stream took on a more desolate hue every day. It was as if the Eternal Father were in agreement with the Trader. There was no rain from the end of May on.

The harvest slowly burned. Large cracks opened up on the dry and thirsty land. Seen from a distance, only the cornfields of Pilato and Ranocchia seemed exceptional, but it was only appearance. The leafy parts of the corn were developed, but the kernels were small and thin and there were not many of them; it would have been more useful as forage for the cattle. The fields belonging to Michele Zompa, Baldovino and me, which had been planted to beans, met a harder fate; they were like weeds burned in the sun. It looked as if a torrent of lava had passed over the gardens of Barletta, Venerdì Santo, Braciola and Papasisto.

It meant famine for Fontamara because the products of the other lands we owned or rented usually served to pay the taxes, rent and other expenses, while the products of the irrigated fields furnished us with food—corn bread and vegetable soup. The theft of the water condemned us to a winter without bread or soup. Was it possible? None of us even tried to get used to such an idea. But whom could we turn to?

The swindle of the ten lustra, coming right after the swindle of the three quarters and three quarters, had opened the eyes even of the blind. On both of these occasions we had been deliberately cheated by the men to whom we had always entrusted our interests. We could depend on no one. It is not easy to explain what that meant to us, collectively and individually. A poor village like Fontamara would be considered helpless without the protection of a "gentleman," possibly a lawyer, to whom every inhabitant knew that he could come to obtain redress from the offenses of some neighboring village, to find work, to emigrate, to obtain a few days' leave for a soldier or to ask for advice in cases of death, marriage and the like.

Nobody from Fontamara would ever have dared to show up in a public office, even to ask for a birth certificate, without being accompanied by don Circostanza. If he had come alone, they would have kicked him out as if he were a dog in church. Baldissera remembered that in the first days of the railroad from Rome to Pescara the people of Fontamara would go to the station at Fossa not only with enough money for the ticket but also with an introduction from don Circostanza. But later there were more train trips and the trains got more and more crowded, so that this was no longer done, and some peasants got as far as Rome without consulting don Circostanza. For the rest, a poor peasant without some "gentleman" as a protector was like a sheep without a shepherd.

But times had been different within the memory of the old people. At one time there had been only three or four proprietors in our region, including a bishop who owned all the land and governed everything according to the three very stable laws that everyone knew. We weren't well off. As a matter of fact, we were very badly off. But everything was simple. According to the old people, the complications and swindles came in with the Piedmontese. Every day they made a new law, and every day they set up a new office. And to keep informed about all this you had to consult lawyers. Theoretically, the law didn't belong to the proprietors any more. It was supposed to be the same for everybody. However, to apply it and to transform it into tyranny the number and importance of the lawyers steadily increased. At the same time the old type of proprietor or priest had declined a great deal, as was shown by don Carlo Magna and don Abbacchio.

When I was a boy there were just two lawyers at Fossa and they did all the notary work too. Now there are eight of them, as well as four notaries, not including the minor swindlers who help settle cases out of court. Since there are so many lawyers, they are forced, just to stay alive, to think up something new every week, to encourage all suits and to drag out at great length the most insignificant of litigations. The quarrels that were once amicably settled now, because of the lawyers, take years, cost a great deal of money and leave behind hate and rancor. Because of the lawyers the relations between families are getting more and more mistrustful. The lawyers are getting involved in everything. And how can you shake loose from them? Their gestures, the tone of their voices, the way they dress, eat and drink seem especially prepared to catch the fancy of the poor. It is every peasant's ambition to have a lawyer as godfather. Thus on confirmation day you can see whole groups of peasants' sons around every lawyer, surrounded by their festively dressed mothers.

The only ones outside these groups are the peasants who have nothing to protect, nothing to lose or gain—the peasants without land. That's true if they aren't criminals, who would need more protection than the others. Needless to say, this protection is never exercised against the rich.

How many times don Circostanza had already swindled us! But how could we live without him? Furthermore, he had such a friendly way about him. He shook hands with all of us, and when he was drunk he even embraced us and asked for our pardon; and we had always forgiven him. But the swindle of three quarters and three quarters and of the ten lustra had depressed us too much.

Nobody could resign himself to the loss of the water—that is, to starvation. But nobody knew what to do about it. Pilato and Michele Zompa wanted us to sue the Trader, but I and some other interested people were opposed to the idea. We knew too well how trials like that ended up. They lasted decades and even centuries; they passed from judge to judge and from appeal to appeal; they ate up the resources of entire villages and finished by leaving everything just as it had been. Even if we had started a suit, whom would we have entrusted it to? Don Circostanza? He would have thought up some other swindle like three quarters and three quarters or the ten lustra. It was better not to discuss it. But all the same, nobody could resign himself to the loss of the water. Nobody could resign himself to the loss of the entire harvest. Nobody could resign himself to the idea of a whole winter with no bread and no soup.

"We're through!" repeated Zompa. "You'll see. One of these days the Lord God will lose patience; there'll be an earthquake. Then there'll be no more talk."

"When the laws of the government aren't any good any more and when the ones who should enforce them are the first to break them, then we go back to the law of the people," replied Baldissera indignantly.

"What is the law of the people?" someone asked him.

"God helps those who help themselves!" said Baldissera, who had ended up by embracing Berardo Viola's bitter doctrine. "Let him who would understand, understand!"

Nobody could prove him wrong, but there was nothing to do about it. Besides, he wouldn't have hurt a fly, even though he did talk like that.

Berardo, instead, said nothing. Poor Berardo wasn't himself any more because he had other things to worry about. The change in him alarmed the boys who thought of him as their leader. His absence the day the water was divided was considered a betrayal, and there was more bitterness against him than against don Circostanza. Berardo led a solitary life and was seldom seen. Now he went from one extreme to the other; all our projects to defend our rights left him indifferent.

"All the worse for you," he sometimes said. "I have no land to irrigate," he said at other times. "I'm not a boy any more," he also said. "I have my own affairs to worry about."

By this time Berardo was obsessed by just one idea—to emigrate, to get away, to work like a dog, to work twice as much as the others, and after six months or a year to come back to Fontamara, buy some land and get married. It was impossible to discuss anything else with him. He wasn't the man he once had been, and I was one of the few who sympathized with him.

"To work ten hours a day, twelve hours a day,

fourteen hours a day," he repeated to me. "Then to
come back with a thousand lire. Ten lire a day isn't
a lot," Berardo said to me. "But that's the average
wage. If I work more, I can make more money. And
as for my expenses, I'll draw in my belt to the last
notch."

Every once in a while he went to don Circostanza's office to see whether some good news about
a job had come from Rome, and he went there
at night to avoid painful discussions with the others.
The lawyer showed a great deal of interest in his
departure and gave him good advice, congratulat-
ing him every now and then on his decision to save
up and get married.

"There's nothing better for driving these foolish
ideas from your head!" he said in his semi-
paternal voice, imitating the speech of a curate.
"A wife, some children, a little house and some
money saved up are much better for keeping young
men like you in hand than fear of the police. I led
a pretty wild life myself," he added in a confiden-
tial tone, "when I was young."

At these words Berardo forgot all the previous
swindles and was reinforced in his decision. Finally, one evening the People's Friend suddenly
summoned him to his office and introduced him to
a Roman businessman. The stranger gave him some
information on finding work in the capital.

"And if the policemen make me get off the train?"
asked Berardo.

"Well, hell, don't tell them you're looking for work!" exclaimed the stranger, laughing at so stupid an objection. "Tell 'em you're on a pilgrimage or that you're going to visit some dying relative at the hospital."

Berardo asked me for a loan of a hundred lire to go, and I gave it to him on the condition that he take my son along. Berardo accepted.

The night before he left, I looked for Berardo to give him some instructions about my son, and I found him in Elvira's shop, sitting on the straw bed where poor Damiano was stretched out.

"I don't want my son to work more than ten hours a day on heavy work!" I began telling Berardo. "I don't want him to go to places where bad women go."

But I had to stop when Raffaele Scarpone came in. He brought in some people who had been waiting for him outside the door.

"The revolution has come to Sulmona," exclaimed Scarpone, turning to Berardo as soon as he came in.

"What revolution?" asked Berardo unenthusiastically.

"What do you mean 'what revolution'?"

"The fudgemakers' revolution?" asked Berardo, laughing.

"The peasants have revolted at Sulmona," explained Scarpone with a no-nonsense tone in his voice.

"Who told you this?" asked Berardo mistrustfully.

Scarpone hesitated a little, then said:

"Baldissera."

"And who told Baldissera?"

"It's a secret," answered Scarpone.

"Then it's not true!" concluded Berardo, and he turned to continue our interrupted conversation.

Scarpone went out into the street and called Venerdì Santo, who was waiting outside, and told him to bring the shoemaker.

Nobody as much as breathed while we were waiting.

Baldissera made them coax him a long time, then he came, greeted Damiano with great ceremony and told us the following story:

"Today I went to Fossa to buy a piece of sole leather. I met donna Clorinda on the square as she was coming out of the church. As you know, I served in their house as a boy, and there's always been a certain confidence between us, and we still say hello when we meet.

" 'Sant' Antonio sent you here,' said don Carlo Magna's wife to me in a low voice. 'Come up to the house a minute so we can talk.'

"Knowing my duty and having not the vaguest idea of what it was all about, I went to her as soon as I had bought the leather.

" 'Have you heard the news?' she asked me, having opened the door herself. 'There's a revolution at Sulmona. The policemen from here and the nearby villages have been called in as reinforcements.'

"According to her story, it seems that there's a sort of Trader at Sulmona too, who has reduced everyone to misery. The revolution broke out three days ago at the marketplace and is still going on.

" 'Do you think the time has come for our brigand?' she asked, alluding to our Trader. But I didn't say a word. 'For two months I've been keeping two candles burning in front of the statue of Sant' Antonio to bring him bad luck, but nothing has happened yet,' she whispered in my ear. Since I still didn't say anything, she opened up and told me, 'This is the time to act. All the policemen have gone to Sulmona. There's a general feeling against the Trader. Everything's ready to begin. Give the signal. But only Fontamara can do it. When I saw you in front of the church just now, I realized that it was Sant' Antonio who sent you.'

"I explained to her that I had come to town because I wanted to buy some sole leather, but she had something else on her mind.

" 'No! No! It's Sant' Antonio who sent you,' she told me. 'This morning while I was at my prayers the Saint inspired me. He can't do anything for you, however. Only Fontamara can give that brigand the lesson he deserves,' she said. 'And I found you right outside the church.' "

Don Carlo Magna's wife had given the old shoe-

maker to understand that if Fontamara had need of
something, like some gasoline or some guns, it
would be given, as long as it was requested by some
responsible person.

"What do you think of that?" asked Scarpone of
Berardo as soon as Baldissera had finished.

"What do you think of it?" asked Berardo.

"Before we came to your place a lot of us got
together. In the name of the ones who are waiting
outside in the street, I tell you that we should
follow the example of Sulmona and that we
shouldn't refuse help from anyone," answered
Scarpone firmly.

He had already thought up a plan for a night attack, which was to begin with the destruction of the
various establishments belonging to the Trader.

"And what's all that for?" objected Berardo, as
if in a dream.

"Do you live on the moon?" answered Scarpone
angrily. "Don't you know all the Trader has done
to us? Don't you see there's no other way to get
justice? Don't you realize that next winter there
won't be anything but rocks to eat at Fontamara?"

Berardo let him go on. Then with the same
impassivity and pretended ingenuousness he asked
Baldissera:

"If donna Clorinda has something against the
Trader, why does she apply to Sant' Antonio?
Doesn't she have a husband? And if Sant' Antonio
shares her feelings, why does he apply to Fonta-

mara? Doesn't he have angels at his disposal?"

Berardo turned to Scarpone and said in the same tone:

"If you burn up the Trader's establishments, do you think we can eat their ashes next winter? If the workers in the cement factory, in the brick factory and in the tannery are all unemployed, do you think it will do Fontamara any good?"

Finally he changed his tone and made clear what he really felt.

"As a matter of fact, that's not my concern," he remarked. "Our situation is certainly awful. Every-one will have to take care of his own affairs. In the past I have worried too much about other people's business. The result is that at the age of thirty I own nothing more than the straw I sleep on. I'm not a boy any more, and I have to take care of my own affairs. So leave me alone."

"It's not us who won't leave you alone," answered Scarpone. "It's the Trader."

Berardo listened, shaking his head. He knew all these arguments. He had taken this position in hun-dreds of discussions with other peasants. But he was no boy and couldn't risk his life and liberty so thoughtlessly, because he was now no longer alone. Now he had to think differently. And he did think differently. When the whole village had ended up thinking as he formerly did, Berardo had changed his way of thinking.

"Listen," he said, explaining himself better

and speaking in a tone of voice that left no room for doubt. "I don't want to go to jail for your water and your land. I have to take care of my own affairs."

Scarpone and Baldissera got up and left.

In a loud voice—so that we could hear it too—Scarpone said to the boys who were waiting outside in the street:

"Berardo's scared!"

What could happen? Berardo was a god to the boys of Fontamara. Under him they would have gone to their death. It was easy to see that no one would dare to try anything without him.

During the entire discussion Elvira had remained standing near the door and had said nothing. She hadn't taken her eyes off Berardo. At first she had followed him with curiosity; then as if she doubted that he were serious; then with astonishment; and finally, when there was no more room for doubt, with great anxiety—without daring, however, to interrupt or contradict him in the presence of others. But as soon as Scarpone and Baldissera had gone, she couldn't help saying to Berardo in a reproachful tone:

"If you're acting that way for my sake, remember that I began to love you when they told me that you thought the other way."

When he realized that even Elvira was against him, he couldn't resist a gesture of anger and was perhaps about to say something obscene. But he pre-

ferred to go away without taking leave of anyone.

When I got back home, I found my wife and son
waiting for me.

My wife had given my son one of my old suits
so he wouldn't make a bad impression in Rome.
It was a little wide in the shoulders, but the rest
of it fitted him. To tell the truth, that suit must have
been at least ten years old; still, it was the best we
had in the house. My wife sewed an emblem of San
Giuseppe da Copertino between the lining and the
material of the collar to protect my son from bad
luck. The knapsack behind the door was filled with
food for the first few days: some bread, a couple of
onions, some tomatoes, a handful of almonds and
a little cheese. I gave the boy a letter of recom-
mendation from don Circostanza. It was two years
old, but in case of emergency it was vague enough
for the purpose. I had used it several times and it
was still useful.

"Is there truth in all those stories of revolution?"
asked my wife.

"What's going to happen's going to happen," I
said to my son. "Get to sleep, because tomorrow
you'll have to get up before dawn."

We tried to sleep, or pretended to, and nobody
could. All three of us were still awake when about
two o'clock the church bells suddenly began to ring.
The first two strokes were close enough, while the
others were as echoes of them.

"Did you hear that?" asked my wife, alarmed, turning to me.

"It's a prayer for Mary," I answered. "Let's get to sleep."

But it was an evasive answer.

We all listened, holding our breath. We didn't hear anything else.

About half an hour later we heard two or three more strokes, weaker than the first.

"Did you hear that?" asked my wife, alarmed.

"It's the wind," I answered. "Let's try to sleep."

But the air was still and it couldn't have been the wind. Besides, not even the strongest of winds had been able to ring our church bells.

A little while later there was another peal, which we heard only because we were listening for it.

"It's probably an owl," I said, just for the sake of saying something.

"Can an owl ring church bells?"

"If it's not an owl, it's a weasel," I answered.

"What would a weasel be doing in the church tower?"

"If it's not a weasel, it's a witch," was all I could think of to say.

At that moment in Fontamara there were few people who could sleep. And probably everyone who had been kept awake by this unusual ringing had gone through the same suppositions and discussions. But everyone wanted to mind his own business and nobody got up to see what was going on in the church tower.

My son will tell you what happened next.

8.

At four in the morning Berardo and I left Fontamara and set out for Fossa to take the train to Rome.

Berardo was in an awful mood and didn't answer me when I said good morning. But I pretended not to notice it, so as not to start anything just as we were leaving.

"Did you hear the church bells last night?" I asked him, just for the sake of conversation. It was as if I had talked to the wind.

When we got to the Chapel of the Madonna of the Flood, I tried again:

"Did you hear the church bells?" I asked.

But he didn't answer.

He walked fast, with long steps, and I had all I could do to keep up.

Coming into Fossa, we were surprised by the train whistle, and we ran up to catch the train. It was a freight train. We had a long time to wait for ours.

We had been in the waiting room for half an hour when Scarpone appeared in the door.

Berardo pretended not to see him, turned his back on him and began reading a poster with exaggerated attention. Scarpone came up to him:

"Teofilo has hanged himself!" he said to Berardo.

Berardo didn't take his eyes off the poster.

"He was found this morning by Baldissera on the stairs of the church tower," continued Scarpone. "He had the church bell rope tied around his neck.

The body was still warm. He must have swung from that rope all night—and nobody came to help him."

"May he rest in peace," said Berardo without turning.

"I went to the priest," continued Scarpone as if he didn't credit Berardo's impassivity. "I've just come from don Abbacchio's house. First of all he covered me with insults because I woke him so early, then he refused to come and give absolution to Teofilo's body. How could he have refused to give a blessing to a sacristan who had worked all his life for the church? I asked him, 'If you hang yourself, you go to Hell?' He answered, 'And if a sacristan hangs himself, he goes all the more deeply into Hell!'"

"May he rest in peace," repeated Berardo without any alarm.

"We're going to put Teofilo's body in the middle of the church," Scarpone went on, "and keep it there so the Madonna, San Rocco, Sant' Antonio, San Guiseppe da Copertino, San Berardo and all the other saints can have time to look at it and see what condition we're reduced to."

"May he rest in peace," repeated Berardo.

Our train came.

"Don't go!" said Scarpone all of a sudden.

"Why not?" answered Berardo, astonished.

"Don't go!" begged Scarpone.

Berardo started for the train. I followed him,

but my heart wasn't in it. Scarpone followed behind me, shaking his head. Tears were running down his face.

"Today the police are coming to Fontamara for Teofilo," said Scarpone. "Berardo, don't go! Don't leave us! You can go tomorrow!"

But we went.

On the train we didn't exchange one word during the entire trip. Berardo was seated in front of me and looked out the window all the time, as if his whole mind were devoted to one idea.

Looking at him, I understood that Berardo was ready to do anything for success. No scruple would have held him back. He wouldn't have hesitated to throw me out of the window if he had thought it would do him any good. Looking at his jaw made me afraid. If he gets hungry, he'll eat me, I thought.

Through the window you could see, as they raced by, mountains, meadows, houses, gardens, fields, streams, pines, horses, cows, sheep, villages and land. Lots of land.

"So much land," murmured Berardo through his teeth.

Suddenly we realized that two policemen had come into our car and were questioning every traveler.

"Where are you going?" they asked us arrogantly.

"Pilgrimage!" answered Berardo, showing them

a letter from don Abbacchio with the parish seal.

"Have a good trip!" they said.

Berardo smiled.

Before we got off at the station in Rome, Berardo tied his shoelaces and spat on the palms of his hands like one who is ready to knock down any obstacle.

At Rome we got a room at the Inn of the Repentant Thief, which the traveler in don Circostanza's office had recommended to Berardo. On the door of the inn there was a sign that represented the three crosses of Calvary. You might think this meant that the name of the place referred to the famous thief who was crucified on Christ's right, who recognized His divinity and as a reward had the promise, "Today thou shalt be with me in Paradise." But actually the Inn of the Repentant Thief, as we found out later, took its good name from the experience of the proprietor, who, after having been several times in jail for thievery, had as he entered the golden years put himself at the service of the Fascists. He had taken part in numerous punitive expeditions against the enemies of the government, specializing in patriotic thievery, stealing at the expense of the workers' cooperatives and their administration, and doing it so well that at a solemn patriotic ceremony the head of the police himself had given him the title of the Repentant Thief.

The next morning we went to the office that was to send us to work on irrigation. A uniformed doorkeeper sent us to the fourth floor. We went up and found a corridor full of people waiting. We lined up behind the others. About noon our turn came, and only then did we find out that we had lined up not on the fourth, but on the fifth floor.

The next day we came back to the fourth floor. We waited for three hours, seated on a bench, just the two of us. The people of whom we inquired answered back rudely. Finally we were sent to the sixth floor. On the sixth floor we waited until they gave us a new address.

That was how we spent our third day. At the new office they asked us:

"Do you have papers?"

"What papers?" we asked, surprised.

I took out don Circostanza's old letter, which my father had given me. But the clerk laughed at me.

"That won't do," he said. "You have to have papers."

We were taken to a window where a clerk gave us two pieces of paper and pasted twelve stamps on them, one for every month of the year.

"Thirty-five lire," said the clerk.

"Pay! There's always something to pay!" answered Berardo.

We would have suffered as much from thirty-five blows of a stick. We paid the thirty-five lire and came back to the first office with the two pieces of paper.

"Here are the papers," we said.

"You have done your duty," he answered. "To-morrow you can go to the employment office, and declare yourselves unemployed and volunteer for work on irrigation."

So passed our fourth day.

I must say that Berardo didn't seem at all annoyed by all this rigmarole. As a matter of fact, he tried to find it natural.

"The harder a job is to find, the better it pays," he kept saying to me.

In the afternoon when the offices were closed, Berardo took me all over the city.

"Look! Look!" he said to me the first time we came to a house with a sign on it showing it was a bank. Berardo stared at the writing as if he were bewitched.

"There's where the Trader gets his money," he said in my ear.

But further on we found another bank and after that a third and then a fourth, until we couldn't count them any more. Which one belonged to the Trader? It was hard to tell. In the center of Rome where we thought Saint Peter was, there were nothing but banks.

"Look! Look!" said Berardo to me every time we came to a new bank.

Each bank was bigger than the one before, and some of them had cupolas like the churches. Around them was a great hive of people and automobiles.

Berardo never got tired of admiring things.

"But they have cupolas!" I objected. "Maybe they're churches!"

"Yes, but to another God," answered Berardo, laughing. "The God who really rules on earth is Money. And it rules everyone, even priests like don Abbacchio who talk about the God in Heaven. Maybe we were ruined by believing in the old God while the new one rules on earth."

Berardo stopped at every fountain to drink, like the donkeys going to Fucino in the morning, but we ran into enormous fountains that threw huge jets of water into the air, and you couldn't drink out of these.

"Look at all that water wasted," complained Berardo. "If we had all that water at Fontamara . . ."

One day Berardo bought a colored shawl, a comb and a hair clip from a peddler.

"I'll send them to Elvira as soon as I can," he said to me, forcing himself to pronounce that name. "Do you think they'll suit her?"

"Certainly," I answered. Then I added the usual. "Everything suits a beautiful girl."

"Do you really think she's beautiful?" he asked me. "When you are in love," he said, "everything slowly changes its meaning."

Berardo got a big kick out of sitting on benches and in public gardens.

"Sit down," he said to me. "It seems incredible, but it's free."

He used to listen carefully to what people on our bench or on the next one were saying.

"Maybe we'll hear someone say, 'I've been looking all over for a strong reliable workman, possibly from the mountains of Abruzzi, in other words, not a loafer.'"

One night, we found a big crowd of people in front of our inn. A military carriage had lost a wheel and had fallen over on one side against a wall. Several people were trying to put it right side up. They weren't getting anywhere, and (like a lot of city people) they were doing more talking than pushing. Berardo came up, took off his jacket and hat, got down under the wagon and slowly raised up the part that was touching the earth, holding it there while the driver put on the wheel and all of those present admired.

This restored some of his old loquacity.

"Donna Clorinda keeps two candles lit in front of the statue of Sant' Antonio to destroy the power of the banks. Isn't it silly?" he asked me that evening.

But I didn't feel like talking. I knew Berardo wanted to take up the discussion he had had with Scarpone the night before we left. This was very much on his mind, but there wasn't much point in talking about it with me.

"This kind of thing is all right as long as you're a boy," he told me. "Roasting chestnuts is always good for something, but, seriously, what good would it do to burn up the Trader's villa?"

I let him talk because he seemed to need it.

"It's not a question of courage, you understand. How can Scarpone think I'm afraid? It's not a question of courage. If I had some reason to risk my life to make more money than the others, I'd do it. Now I feel I can do what no man ever did before! Understand? You'll see! Tomorrow they'll give us work, and as soon as the work begins, you'll see, and the others will see, the engineers will see."

"How do you suppose Teofilo's funeral went?" I asked, to keep him talking about Fontamara.

He didn't like that at all.

"It's not a question of courage, I tell you," he answered rudely. "It isn't strength. Did the Trader use violence against us? Not at all. The Trader has used neither courage nor strength, but shrewdness. That's how he took the stream. As a matter of fact, he didn't even take it. Fontamara gave it to him. The men signed a petition to the government, then they accepted the swindle of three quarters and three quarters, then the one about the ten lustra. What was the Trader supposed to do? The Trader just acted correctly for his own interests."

That's how confused he was.

"Certainly the price of land will go down," he

went on, showing his innermost thoughts. "Without water the price will go down, and the land will
change hands."

He already knew what land he wanted to buy
when he got back. But he wouldn't tell me which
land it was.

The morning of the fifth day we went to the employment office to get jobs.

"What province are you from?" they asked us
after we had waited all morning in front of a
window.

"From the province of Aquila," we answered.

"In that case you'll have to go to the office for
Aquila," they answered.

"Where is the office for Aquila?" we asked.

The clerk burst out laughing. He told the other
clerks what we'd asked and the laughter spread
through all the office. When calm was restored and
the clerk had dried his eyes, which were wet with
laughter, he explained to us:

"The office for Aquila is in Aquila."

But we didn't want to make a tour of Italy.

"We've already seen too many offices!" said Berardo in an energetic tone. "We came to Rome with
an introduction from a lawyer to be given work on
irrigation, not to undertake this *Via Crucis*."

The clerk closed the window in our faces, and the
Via Crucis continued.

At the Inn of the Repentant Thief there lived a
lawyer from Abruzzi, the Cavaliere don Achille

Pazienza. On the advice of the Repentant Thief, we went to him, and the following day, the sixth of our stay in Rome, he received us in his bedroom, which was next to ours and similar for its darkness, narrowness, disorder and dirt. We found don Achille Pazienza stretched out on the bed. He was a poor little old man with a cold, with ten days of beard, a yellow suit, white cloth shoes, a straw hat on his head, a bronze medal on his chest and a wooden toothpick in his mouth. That was how he received us. There was a well-filled chamber pot under the bed. On the darkest wall there was a phosphorescent portrait in yellow and green, under which was written *Duce*.

"The consultation costs ten lire," began don Pazienza.

"All right!" I answered impulsively.

"Ten lire in advance," added the Cavaliere.

We gave him ten lire.

"Ten lire each," said the Cavaliere.

We gave him another ten lire.

Then the Cavaliere got up from the bed and went out of the room without saying anything to us. We heard him coughing in the corridor. Then we heard the cough go slowly down the stairs, stop for a while on the ground floor, where the Repentant Thief was waiting, go out in the street and die out in a nearby restaurant.

We had to wait almost an hour before the cough

reappeared, recrossed the street, slowly came up the stairs, stopped a while at our door and came in. He threw on the bed behind him a piece of bread, half a salami and half a flask of red wine.

"Your case looks bad," said the Cavaliere Pazienza to us after he had taken up his horizontal position again. He ignored the fact that we hadn't told him what it was all about.

"How much money do you have left?" he asked after a meditative pause.

We put all we had left into Berardo's hat, even copper change, and counted about fourteen lire.

"Your case is insignificant and even desperate," said the disappointed Cavaliere.

After another meditative pause he asked us:

"Couldn't you send to Fontamara for some more money?"

"Certainly," answered Berardo, though he was sure of the contrary.

"And maybe a little hen and some cheese and some honey for my cough?" added the Cavaliere.

"Certainly," Berardo hastened to say (though he had never tasted honey in his life).

"Now your case is clear," said the Cavaliere Pazienza with a huge horselike smile, showing about twenty yellowed teeth.

"Talk!" he ordered us.

Berardo explained why we had come to Rome. The Cavaliere got up, sought out a stick that looked for all the world like an old umbrella handle, and waving it in the air as if he were going off to war, said to us:

"Follow me!"

We followed him. The first stop was at the telegraph office. The Cavaliere wrote out this telegram:

"Need two hundred lire, twenty-five pounds of cheese, five pounds of honey and some hens."

Then he asked us:

"Whom shall I send this telegram to? Which of you has the richest family?"

"Send it to my father, Vincenzo Viola," answered Berardo, who had lost his father when he was a child.

Don Pazienza was about to hand in the telegram when Berardo asked him:

"Cavaliere, do you like peaches?"

"I certainly do," he answered. "They're very good for a cough!"

So we added to the telegram a request for twenty-five pounds of peaches. The Cavaliere made a copy of it, then added to us:

"Pay for it, and follow me."

The second stop was at the employment office from which we had been thrown out the day before. Don Pazienza left us in the hall, but we could see him arguing violently with the head of the office, showing him a copy of the telegram and pointing out the important expressions with his finger. The head of the office must have had some strong objections, because we saw the Cavaliere grow pale. He came up to us and asked:

"Is the cheese at Fontamara for grating or eating?"

"If it's fresh, it's edible; if it's dry, it's for grating," answered Berardo to the great satisfaction of the Cavaliere, who hurried away to give the reassuring answer to the head of the office.

There were no other serious objections, so the Cavaliere came to tell us:

"Things are under way. The office will send out a request for the necessary documents—birth certificates, police reports, good-conduct certificates. As soon as they're here, you'll be enrolled as unemployed. The irrigation work will come later. The office will call you."

On our seventh day in Rome all we had left was four lire. We bought some bread and were left without a single copper.

"Soon we'll be called by the office," Berardo kept repeating to me to give himself courage.

He was still far from despair. Thus one day when he was lying on the bed, he was suddenly taken by a strange delusion. We left the room in a great rush.

He explained to me:

"Someone might stop us on the street and ask us, 'Excuse me, would you be willing to work? Would thirty lire be enough to start? Naturally this would include food and drink. If you want, you can begin tomorrow.'"

We came to a big street and sat down on the first bench we came to, listening to what we heard around us. After a while Berardo snatched at another hope:

"Don Achille Pazienza is probably looking for us," he said to me, "and he's getting madder every minute. He's probably saying, 'Now that I've found work for these people, they've gone away.'"

Because we wanted to be able to come immediately when we were called and also because we didn't feel much like walking—since we hadn't eaten anything—we didn't leave the inn any more. Whenever we heard steps, we ran out. Every time we saw the mailman come, we rushed down to the ground floor, where the Repentant Thief was ensconced.

It must be said that the Cavaliere Pazienza lived in the same anxiety, with the difference, however, that we were waiting to be called to work, and he was waiting for the money order and the appetizing provisions from Berardo's father. All three of us passed the day stretched out on our beds, and all three of us ran downstairs at every sound. As we came back upstairs, the reciprocal recriminations became more and more bitter.

"Your father is unnatural," said the Cavaliere Pazienza to Berardo. "Why doesn't he send the two hundred lire?"

"Is there a job or isn't there?" answered Berardo. "If there is, why don't they call me? If there's work, why are there so many formalities?"

"I know it takes time for the packages," added the Cavaliere Pazienza. "They travel slowly, especially when they have fragile jars in them. But a telegram takes only a day. Your father is stingy."

"Why do you need a birth certificate to work?" continued Berardo. "If someone asks for a job, it's clear that he's already born."

After three days of hunger and useless waiting Berardo and I stopped going down every time the mailman came. We stayed on our beds from morning to night and got up only to drink water from the faucet in the bathroom. The Cavaliere Pazienza showed himself much more optimistic and constant than we did. Three times a day, every time the mailman came, we heard his cough get up from bed, leave the room, slowly go down the stairs to the ground floor. After a while he would slowly and painfully come up, stop at our door and hurl curses through it at the people of Fontamara.

"Berardo Viola, your father is lazy!" complained the poor old man. "Your father is my ruin, Berardo Viola. Your father is my death! I haven't eaten for three days, and it's all your father's fault!" he yelled.

Berardo didn't answer. He had fallen back into silence. He watched the ceiling for hours, without saying a word, stretched out on the bed with his hands folded behind his head.

"What'll we do?" I asked. "We can't always go without eating."

But Berardo didn't answer.

Once he said to me:

"They say that my grandfather, when he was fighting with the mountain, went for three weeks without eating. He drank only water."

Another time he asked me:

"What day is this?" Then he added: "Elvira must have gotten back from the pilgrimage by this time, the one she wanted to make to the Madonna della Livera—a pilgrimage on foot, with poor Maria Grazia, to ask for pardon."

"Elvira has no need of pardon," I said. "She probably went along to keep Maria Grazia company."

On the afternoon of the fourth day of hunger we received good news. It was about five o'clock when we heard the confused cries of the Cavaliere and the Repentant Thief.

"Victory! Victory!" yelled the Cavaliere, singing a patriotic song:

> *O where are the wings of Victory,*
> *Which is held in bondage by Rome?*
> *God made her . . .*

Both of them came to our door and burst in without knocking. The Repentant Thief was waving a telegram in the air. It was for Berardo, and the

Cavaliere was holding a couple of bottles of wine.

"Berardo Viola," yelled the Cavaliere, "your father is a real gentleman. His money has arrived!"

"Really?" said Berardo, beside himself with joy.

How could he possibly have thought that his father, dead for twenty years, could have sent him money? Evidently he had no further desire to think after four days of starvation.

While the Cavaliere was pouring out the wine to celebrate the joyous event, Berardo took the telegram, opened it, read it, read it again, looked at us, folded it up and put it into his pocket without saying a word.

"What is it?" I asked.

Berardo didn't answer. He didn't even hear me. His face took on a frightful expression, and his eyes became numbed and bloodshot.

"What is it?" I asked again, in as friendly a voice as possible.

Berardo got back on the bed without saying a word. The Repentant Thief and the Cavaliere Pazienza went away astonished. I sat down next to Berardo and asked him once more:

"What's happened? Is someone dead?"

But he didn't answer, and I don't know how I guessed that someone he knew at Fontamara was dead.

That evening at about eight there were various unusual noises in the room next to ours that was occupied by the Cavaliere Pazienza. He said to us from our door:

"The head of the employment office came by. Your certificates have arrived. On the certificate of morality from the podestà it is written: 'Extremely unpatriotic conduct.' With a certificate like that you'll never get a job. What's more, the police have been informed. You'll never get any work."

He closed the door and went away.

Five minutes later the door was opened again.

"Your room has been rented," said the Repentant Thief to us. "You have half an hour to leave it."

It was already dark when they threw us out of the Inn of the Repentant Thief.

"What'll we do now?" I asked Berardo.

But what could he answer? He didn't say anything. I felt very weak in the legs, and I was so hungry that I had a terrible headache. Every once in a while I thought I was going to fall. The people passing in the streets turned to look at us; the gentlemen stepped aside as if they were afraid of us. And Berardo really looked frightful.

There were many watermelon stands on the streets surrounded by all sorts of people who were making noises to show how happy they were. Some of the stands were surmounted with arches of colored lights. In the gardens of the restaurants there were several couples dancing who must certainly have already eaten.

"We can ask for soup in some convent," I proposed to Berardo.

But he didn't answer.

In this way, silently, we came just by chance to the neighborhood of the station. On the square there were a large number of policemen and soldiers who stopped the passers-by and searched them. A young man looked at us with astonishment and came forward.

"Good evening," he said to Berardo, laughing.

Berardo looked at him distrustfully and didn't answer.

"I was thinking of you," added the young man. "If I hadn't met you here, I would have gone to look for you at Fontamara."

"I haven't a cent," Berardo said. "If you want to cheat somebody, you'd better choose someone else."

The young man laughed. He looked half student and half workman. He was tall and thin, well dressed but not elegantly, and his voice and manner inspired confidence.

"Do you remember the last time you were at Avezzano?" asked the young man. "Do you remember the restaurant where the redheaded policeman brought you? Do you remember? But you've forgotten that I warned you about him."

Berardo took a good look and recognized the young man.

"Buy us some food!" I asked him when I saw

that Berardo was going to let the chance go by.

The young man brought us into a place near the station and ordered some eggs and some ham.

"Who's going to pay for us?" asked Berardo mistrustfully. "We haven't a lira left."

To reassure Berardo the young man had to go to the cashier and pay for the food in advance. Meanwhile, Berardo looked at me as if to tell me that the man was crazy.

"What are all those soldiers and policemen for?" asked Berardo after he had eaten something.

"They're looking for the Solitary Stranger," he answered.

But the answer wasn't very clear.

"For some time a stranger, the Solitary Stranger, has been endangering the public order," added the young man in a low voice. "At all the trials before the special tribunal they talk of the Solitary Stranger. He prints and distributes clandestine newspapers that denounce scandals, incite the workmen to strike and the citizens to disobey. Those who are found with illegal printed matter always confess that they got it from the Solitary Stranger. In the beginning he liked to work around certain factories; then he began operating in the suburbs of the city and the military barracks; finally he showed up at the University. On the same day he is discovered in several different provinces and even at the frontier. The best detectives have been looking for him, but they haven't caught him yet. Several thousand people have been arrested, and some-times the government thought it had the Solitary Stranger among those arrested. But after a short interruption the clandestine press took up its work again and the *Judicial Gazette* once more dis-cussed the activities of the Solitary Stranger. It has seemed for some time that he's been going to Abruzzi."

"To Abruzzi?" asked Berardo with agitation.

"At Sulmona, at Prezza, at Avezzano and at other places. Wherever the peasants revolt he goes."

"But who is this fellow? Is he the Devil?" asked Berardo.

"Maybe he is," answered the man from Avez-zano. "But he's a good devil."

"If I could tell him how to get to Fonta-mara . . ." said Berardo.

"He already knows the way," answered the other in a low voice.

At that moment a policeman, followed by a group of soldiers, entered the place and came up to us.

"Passports or identity cards!" he demanded arrogantly.

While the policeman examined the papers that Berardo and I had got from the employment office, as well as the identity card, the passport and several other documents belonging to the man from Avez-zano, the soldiers searched the restaurant.

Our papers were in order and the policeman was about to leave when the soldiers ran up to him, showing him a package wrapped in cloth that they had found under the coatrack. When they saw what was inside the package, the policeman and the soldiers jumped up as if they had been bitten by a tarantula, and threw themselves on us, yelling:

"Whose package is this? Who left this on the floor?"

And without even hearing what we answered they took us off to the police station.

Berardo thought that we had been taken for thieves and that the package found on the floor contained stolen goods, so that when we came into the police station he began to yell over and over:

"Thieves? Us? You should be ashamed of yourselves! You're the thieves! We're victims, not thieves! The thieves are the men at the employment office! They took thirty-five lire from us! Cavaliere Pazienza is a thief! He took twenty lire from us. Thieves? Us? The Trader is a thief, but you wouldn't dare arrest him!"

In the police station where they took us, groups of people they had arrested kept coming in from various parts of the city.

"They're still looking for the Solitary Stranger!" the man from Avezzano explained to Berardo in a low voice. Berardo had finally realized that we weren't suspected of being thieves and had calmed down.

When, after very little ceremony, we were locked up in a dark cell where there were two other prisoners, Berardo and I exchanged a smile of satisfaction; we finally had a place to sleep and some food for tomorrow assured. As far as the future went, we would have time to think later.

Half the cell was occupied by a cement platform a little bit higher than the floor, and this platform served as a bed. In a corner was a hole whose function was even more evident. Two prisoners who had preceded us to the cell were crouched in a corner with their heads on jackets that had been folded to form cushions. I followed their example. I took off my jacket, lay down on the cement and folded the jacket under my head. But Berardo and the man from Avezzano began a lively discussion, pacing back and forth in the cell. The man from Avezzano spoke in a low voice, perhaps out of mistrust for the two strangers, but Berardo couldn't keep his voice down. Therefore I could hear only what Berardo said during the whole discussion.

"This business about the Solitary Stranger doesn't convince me," he said. "Is the Solitary Stranger a townsman or a peasant? If he is a townsman and comes to Abruzzi, he must be working some swindle!"

The man from Avezzano laughed.

"But the people in the city are well off," Berardo next said. "The city people are well off because they take advantage of the peasants. I know that there are some people in the city who aren't well off. For example, the Cavaliere hardly has money to burn. However, he isn't really from the city. He's from Abruzzi and he moved to the city."

Sometimes Berardo would try to speak low, and I entirely lost the thread of their conversation. But his gestures and those of the man from Avezzano made it obvious that they had come to no agreement. When he really should have spoken in a low voice, Berardo got excited, and not only the prisoners in our cell but also the ones in the cells next door could hear him.

"All they found in that package was some newspapers. And did they arrest all these people for a package of paper? What is a package of paper worth?"

The man from Avezzano warned Berardo to speak softly, and Berardo agreed. Then he raised his voice again.

"A union of city people and peasants? But the city people are well off and the peasants aren't; the city people work less and make more money; they eat and drink well, and they don't pay any taxes. Just look at how much they make us pay for hats, cloth and leather. We are like worms. Everybody takes advantage of us. Everybody oppresses us. Everybody swindles us. Even don Circostanza. Even him."

The man from Avezzano listened patiently.

"I don't understand!" Berardo kept repeating. "I don't understand why the city people can distribute a free newspaper to the peasants. Why doesn't the Solitary Stranger mind his own business? Maybe he sells paper and prints the newspapers to advertise his business!"

The other tried to make him lower his voice.

"Are all these people you talk about who go to prison crazy?" I heard Berardo saying. "And if they've gone crazy, what good does it do them? And the ones who get shot? What good did it do them? Is that how to mind your business—get yourself shot?"

From what I could understand, the stranger was trying to get at Berardo through his pride. He said:

"I can understand how the other peasants can't comprehend certain things—but a person like yourself!"

To Berardo's every argument he repeated, "A man like you! You *can't* believe what you're saying."

The man from Avezzano must have realized that most of Berardo's objections were made to himself. The hopes that Berardo had when he left Fontamara had all vanished. There was no longer any possibility of his attending to his own affairs, of finding work and getting some land. All the chances had gone.

The podestà had defined us as men of the worst possible conduct, and therefore, the Cavaliere Pazienza assured us, no possibility remained. The objections Berardo made to the man from Avezzano were his last resistance.

Later the conversation took up other countries, even Russia, for at one point I heard Berardo saying:

"Russia? Tell me the truth. Is there really this Russia that everybody is talking about? Everybody talks about it, but no one has been there. The peasants, as a matter of fact, go everywhere—to America, to Africa, to France. But none of them ever got to Russia."

Berardo was adamant on some points, as when they spoke of freedom.

"Free speech?" asked Berardo in a sneering tone. "But we're not lawyers. Freedom of the press? But we're not publishers. Why don't you talk about freedom to work, freedom to own land?"

Then without knowing it I dozed off. I had been asleep several hours when Berardo woke me up. He was seated at my feet, and the man from Avezzano was near him. I was surprised that they were still awake and talking. The man from Avezzano was telling Berardo his life story, all about his childhood and adolescence.

There was no more disagreement. From his way of speaking and gesturing you could tell that Berardo had abandoned all resistance. He was his old self again.

"What's happening?" I asked sleepily. "Why don't you sleep?"

"We've already slept too much," answered Berardo, laughing.

I hadn't seen him laugh for a long time. And his laugh was so extraordinary that it made me afraid. From the way the two of them were talking and smiling, I realized that Berardo had formed a friendship with the stranger, and since I knew what friendship meant to him, I had the vague impression that Berardo was lost.

Then he said something to me under his breath that I'll never forget.

"I thought my life had no more sense for me," he said, "but perhaps now it will have some meaning."

And after a while, he added:

"Maybe it will begin to make sense only now."

"Have you found work?" I asked him.

"Work? What work?" he said.

"Have you forgotten that we came to Rome to find work?" I insisted.

"Go to sleep!" he told me. "We'll talk about it tomorrow."

And I went back to sleep.

When he woke me again, it was already day. Berardo was walking up and down the cell like a caged lion. The man from Avezzano was lying down near me, but he wasn't asleep. He looked as if he were waiting for me to wake up.

"Do you trust Berardo?" he asked me in a low voice.

"Yes," I answered.

"All the peasants should trust him," he added. "You must say this at Fontamara; all the peasants must trust him. He is an extraordinary man. What happened to him just had to happen. There probably isn't another peasant like him in all Italy. You must repeat my words at Fontamara. You must do all that Berardo tells you. You will probably be set free in a few days and will be sent home. It'll be different for me. I'm sorry I can't tell you about it. Berardo will tell you at Fontamara. The first thing to do is to make peace between Berardo and Scarpone. Berardo knows the rest."

At eight o'clock they gave us a bowl of coffee. Berardo stopped walking up and down and said to the jailer:

"I want to talk to the inspector right away."

"Wait for your turn," said the jailer scornfully, slamming the door in Berardo's face.

The man from Avezzano took in every word of this, looking with horror at Berardo. He didn't dare ask for an explanation, but you could see the fear of betrayal on his face.

At nine o'clock they brought all three of us to the inspector.

Berardo came up and said:

"Inspector, I'm ready to tell everything."

"Go ahead," answered the man of the law.

"The package of newspapers found in the restaurant near the station belongs to me. It was I who had them printed. I am the Solitary Stranger."

9.

So they had finally arrested the Solitary Stranger! Several newspapermen and some high functionaries of the state rushed to the police station where we were prisoners at the first rumor that the Stranger, the Solitary Stranger, had been caught. And he was a peasant.

The police had looked for the Stranger in the city, but is there anyone in the city who is really a stranger? Every city man is licensed, catalogued and carefully watched. He is, in short, no stranger. But the peasant? Who knows the peasant? Has there ever been a government that did? Who could ever license, catalogue and carefully watch all the peasants?

So it was not strange that the Stranger, the Solitary Stranger, was a peasant. Every once in a while Berardo was taken from the cell to be shown to some new official who wanted to question the peasant or merely to see the Solitary Stranger with his own eyes. In the evening they gave us three separate cells as a precaution. But during the following days we were all questioned together.

The inspector wanted to know a lot from Berardo. He wanted to know where the clandestine press was, who the printer was, and whether there were any other accomplices. But Berardo didn't answer. Berardo drew his lips in between his teeth and bit them until they bled to show to this inspector his inflexible will not to talk. He always appeared more melancholy in the questioning

periods. The first time he had nothing but a deep
mark under his right eye. But after the question-
ings that followed, his face was hardly recogniza-
ble; the lips, the nose, the eyes and the eyebrows
all carried obvious signs of violence. But he
wouldn't talk. He wouldn't answer the inspector's
questions. Not being able to take his lacerated
lips between his teeth, he clamped his jaw shut as a
sign of his inflexible determination not to talk.

One evening, I had a "special call" too.

"Let's have the truth!" the inspector ordered.

I told him the truth, but he didn't believe me.

I was taken into an underground cell and thrown
onto a wooden bench; my hands were tied behind
my back with leather thongs. Suddenly it was as if
I had fallen into a rain of fire. It was as if my back
had opened up and the fire had gone in. It was as if
I had fallen into a bottomless pit.

When I came to, I saw on the bench the little pud-
dle of blood that had come out of my mouth. I
tasted it with my tongue, and drank a little because
my throat was burning.

The next day the man from Avezzano was set free.

Berardo and I were together again in the same
cell with someone who looked for all the world
like a policeman. I told Berardo about this, but he
answered:

"I don't care. I've said everything I have to say."

But when I told him that the man from Avezzano
had got out, he had an unexpected reaction.

"He has?" he said smiling. "Now we've got to find a way to get out ourselves. Two can play at that game."

It had been easy to begin the game; it was much harder to end it.

When Berardo told the inspector that his first confession had been false, the inspector burst out laughing, sent him back into his cell and said to him:

"If you don't tell us everthing you know, it'll be hard for you."

That same evening Berardo had another "special call." Berardo's special calls must have been something awful. He could never get hit without wanting to hit back, so that it always took eight or nine policemen to tie his hands and feet. That evening he was no longer resigned to torture. While a policeman was tying a rope around his knees, Berardo bit into his neck and held him so firmly that the other policemen had to hammer at his jaws to make him let go. Finally they led him back to the cell, holding him by the arms and legs, like Christ when He was taken off the Cross.

"He's outside and I'm in here," Berardo said to me the next day. "And he is nothing but a city man, after all. He's getting out of all this and I'm getting mangled for his sake. Why shouldn't I tell everything?"

(The prisoner whom we suspected of being a policeman was listening with great interest.)

When we were again called to the inspector, I didn't know if Berardo did well or not to tell everything we had learned from the Avezzano man, just to get out of jail.

"Are you ready to confess everything?" the inspector asked Berardo.

Berardo made an almost imperceptible nod with his head. He could hardly stand on his feet, because of the wounds all over him; his face was unrecognizable.

At this point the inspector opened a drawer and took out a newspaper which carried in large type this headline:

VIVA BERARDO VIOLA

"In this newspaper," said the inspector, "in this anonymous rag, there is something about the treatment justly meted out to you from your arrival up to now. Since you want to confess everything, tell us how you got the information out of the cell to this clandestine sheet."

Berardo didn't answer.

"In this paper," continued the inspector, "there is a lot about Fontamara. There is something about changing the course of a stream, something about a pasture, about the question of Fucino, about the suicide of one Teofilo, and about the death of a girl called Elvira, and other such things. Obviously only someone from Fontamara could give

out such information. Tell me how this happened!"

Berardo didn't answer. He was looking as if
hypnotized at the paper, in which his name and
Elvira's were printed under the headline:

VIVA BERARDO VIOLA

"So talk!" insisted the inspector.

"Impossible, inspector," answered Berardo,
choked with emotion. "I'd rather die."

The inspector continued to press him. But Berardo was already elsewhere in spirit. He didn't
even see the inspector any more. He didn't hear
him. He let himself be brought back into the cell
like one who has just made his will before dying.
But it wasn't over yet.

Neither of us closed his eyes during the night. Berardo held his head in his hands, as if it were about
to explode. He would decide to confess, then repent
of it, decide again, and again repent. He held his
head firmly in his hands to prevent it from explod-
ing. Why did he have to stay in jail? Why did
he have to die in jail at the age of thirty? For honor?
For an ideal? But when had he ever bothered about
politics? Thus the night passed. Thus Berardo
spoke throughout the night, while each of his two
selves tried to weigh every word. The struggle continued:

"Is life worth living, now that Elvira is dead?

And if I betray it, the idea is lost. If I turn traitor, Fontamara will be eternally damned. If I turn traitor, hundreds of years will go by before another chance comes up. And if I die? It will be the first time a peasant dies not for himself but for some-one else."

This was his first great discovery. It opened his eyes wide, as if a great light had entered the cell.

I'll never forget the tone of his voice and the expression of his face while he spoke his last words to me.

"It will be something new," he said. "A new ex-ample. The beginning of something entirely new."

Then he added, remembering something impor-tant:

"From the time I was a boy, it was foreseen that I would die in jail."

This pacified him a great deal. He was stretched out on the cement like a fallen tree, a tree ready for the fire.

He added only:

"Give my regards to my friends when you see them again!"

These were the last words I heard from Berardo.

The following morning we were separated for the last time.

And two days later I was called to the inspector, who was unusually polite.

"Berardo Viola killed himself last night," he

said. "He hanged himself from the window of his cell in desperation. We're sure of this. But nobody was present, and we need an affidavit. If you would sign an affidavit certifying that your friend hanged himself, you could go today."

When I heard that Berardo had been killed, I burst into tears.

The inspector wrote something on a piece of paper, and I signed it without reading it. I would have signed anything, even my own death warrant.

Then I was taken into the office of the chief of police.

"Were you a friend of the late Berardo Viola?" he asked me.

"Yes, sir."

"Do you declare that the deceased had always shown suicidal tendencies?"

"Yes, sir."

"Do you declare that the deceased had recently been gravely disappointed in love?"

"Yes, sir."

"Do you declare that the deceased was in the same cell as yourself and that he had taken advantage of the fact that you were asleep to hang himself from a bar of the window?"

"Yes, sir."

"Good boy," said the inspector, who had been present when I was questioned. He offered me a cigarette as I went out.

Then I was taken to the Justice Department, to

some judge's office. It was the same thing all over again.

"Were you a friend of Berardo Viola, deceased?" the judge asked me. "Do you declare that the deceased had recently been gravely disappointed in love? Do you declare that the deceased was in the same cell with yourself and had taken advantage of the fact that you were asleep to hang himself from a window bar?"

"Yes, sir! Yes, sir! *Yes, sir!*

Then he had me sign a piece of paper and let me go.

At noon they set me free. They took me to the station and put me on the train, with a one-way ticket of compulsory travel.

My father and mother can tell you the rest.

10.

By the time my son got to Fontamara, the Solitary Stranger had told us most of what he had told you.

For old Maria Rosa the news had been awful, as we had foreseen. For a whole night Fontamara resounded with her lamentations.

"My poor son," she cried. "Forgive my bringing you into the world for such a hard fate! And may his bride forgive me if I ruined her with my promises."

Several women, grouped around the grieving mother, seated on the stones in front of her cave, were reciting prayers for the dead.

"He ended up like his grandfather," cried Maria Rosa. "How many times I warned him. I warned him from the time he was a boy. The Violas don't die at home like other Christians. Nobody knows why, but they have never died of coughs or fevers. They can't stay in bed near the hearth. Nobody has ever found out why."

There was also Maria Grazia, the girl who had been raped when they came to examine the people of Fontamara, and she told of her pilgrimage and of Elvira's death.

At first, no one could figure out why Elvira wanted to perform a difficult pilgrimage with Maria Grazia, and some thought it was just to keep her friend company. But when—after a whole day of walking, after the steep, dusty, stony valley of Forca Caruso, after the long gorge of San Venanzio—when the two girls came into the sanctuary of the Madonna della Libera, Maria Grazia understood immediately what Elvira's pilgrimage was all about.

"Most Holy Virgin Mary," said Elvira, as soon as she came to the holy image, "I ask for only one thing: that you intercede for Berardo's salvation. In exchange for this, I offer you the only poor thing which I have—my life. I offer it to you without hesitation, without regret, without reservations."

She had hardly finished saying these words when she was stricken with a high fever. She began to burn up, like a bundle of dry twigs that has been recently kindled. "I offer you my life," repeated Elvira to the sacred image, and feeling that her offer had been accepted, added: "I ask only to be able to die at home." And this boon was granted by the most pitying Virgin. She came back home, put her few things in order, gave her sick father to the care of an aunt, went to bed, and died.

"And was Berardo saved?" a woman murmured.

"Perhaps," said old Maria Rosa. "Nobody can ever know."

"Strange way to die, in jail," said the other in a low voice.

"Nobody will ever know," repeated the mother. "My poor son wasn't born for property, but he wanted to own land at any cost. He was never able to sit still in a chair, but he wanted a house of his own. He who had never tolerated an injustice, who was born for his friends, wanted to stick to his own affairs. I'm his mother, yet I can't tell you the incredible sacrilegious things he said before he left for Rome; he was ready to do anything just to succeed. All for the love of a woman. Maybe her death has saved him."

"Strange way to die, in jail," repeated the other woman between her teeth.

"Nobody will ever know," continued the mother in an angry voice. "Maybe Berardo's salvation consisted in returning to his destiny. The salvation of the Violas has never been the same as that of other Christians. They don't die of coughs or fevers, with a pot full of piss under their bed. Haven't the old people ever told you how his grandfather died? And no one ever did find out how his father died."

"What's all this about the paper that's going to be printed?" asked the Limona woman.

"It's some newfangled idea," answered a girl. "I heard Scarpone telling about it, but I didn't understand a word."

"When the newfangled things start, who's going to stop them?" I asked. "Let's leave these things to the men!"

My son got back just when about ten of us were gathered around a box and some other things the Solitary Stranger had brought us to put out the peasant paper with—as a matter of fact, the first peasant paper of all. On the box was written: POLYGRAPH.

We had innocently put the box on Marietta's table, right in the middle of the street, and we were talking about the paper we were going to put out, about ten of us, as I said. It was newfangled, and we didn't know how newfangled it was.

It was Maria Grazia who had the clearest handwriting, and she was to make the stencil. Baldissera knew the grammar and where to put the apostrophes. Scarpone had learned from the Solitary Stranger how to work the machine.

Our first discussion was about the title of the newspaper.

Baldissera wanted a title like the ones used in the cities: *The Messenger, The Tribune,* or something like that. But Scarpone, who had inherited Berardo's manner, made him stop.

"We're not copying any paper. There's never been a paper like ours before," Scarpone said.

Michele proposed a nice title, *The Truth,* which seemed to mean a lot.

But Scarpone wrinkled his nose.

"Truth?" he said. "Who knows the truth?"

"We don't know it, but we want to know it," answered Michele.

"And when you've found it," Scarpone said, "will it feed you?"

This was the way he thought.

Losurdo had a good idea: *Justice.*

"But you're crazy!" Scarpone said to him. "Justice has always been against us!"

With us, "justice" has always meant the police. Having to do with justice has always meant having to do with the police. Falling into the hands of justice has always meant falling into the hands of the police.

"But I mean real justice," answered Losurdo in an angry mood. "Justice is the same for everybody."

"You'll find that in Heaven," decided Scarpone.

What could you answer to that?

Marietta proposed as the title *The Peasant's Trumpet.*

But nobody discussed her proposal.

"What can we do?" asked Scarpone.

"We have to think up a title," answered Marietta. "You think of something."

"I've thought of it: *What Can We Do?*"

We looked at each other, surprised.

"But it's not a title," Baldissera remarked. "It's not a title. We have to have a title to put on the top of a newspaper, you understand, with an elegant handwriting!"

"All right, write on the top of the paper, with an elegant handwriting, *What Can We Do?*" answered Scarpone. "And that will be the title."

"But it will be a ridiculous title," objected Baldissera. "If a copy of our paper gets to Rome, anyone who sees it will burst out laughing."

Scarpone got furious. The paper had to be a peasant paper, the first peasant paper of all. A paper in handwriting. He didn't care what they thought about it in Rome.

Finally Baldissera was convinced. So Scarpone's proposal was approved.

While Maria Grazia wrote out the title of the paper, we passed on to the title of the first article.

Maria Grazia wrote with her head on her shoulder, like a schoolgirl, and it all looked like a child's game. Funny, I thought to myself. It's funny how many strange things are happening all at once.

Zompa proposed:

"The first headline should say—I think we'll all agree about this—'They've Killed Berardo Viola!' "

Scarpone agreed, but proposed to add something.

" 'They've killed Berardo Viola! What can we do?' "

"That's in the name *What Can We Do?*" observed Michele.

"It's not enough," answered Scarpone. "We should repeat it. If it's not repeated, the title's no good. It would be better to leave it out. 'What can we do?' must be repeated in every article. 'They've taken away our water! What can we do?' 'They rape our women in the name of the law! What can we do?' 'Don Circostanza's good for nothing! What can we do?' "

Then we all understood Scarpone's idea and we agreed with him.

We had another little discussion about Berardo's name. Baldissera thought it should be spelled with two *l*'s, while Marietta thought one would be enough. But Maria Grazia said she could write it so that no one would know whether there was one or two, and that finished the discussion.

When I realized that there was no more to discuss, I left the company and went home to be alone with my son, because I thought I had lost him, and I found him again.

Late that night Scarpone came by my place with thirty copies of the paper *What Can We Do?* for me to distribute at San Giuseppe, where we knew a lot of people. The next day other people were to hand them out in other neighboring villages. In all, five hundred copies had been made.

When my wife saw the papers, she made a wry face.

"Now we're getting like Innocenzo La Legge, who hands out pieces of paper," she said to me.

"Berardo's name is on it," I said. "That's the only reason."

"When the newfangled things start up," replied my wife, "nobody can stop them."

"You're right," I said to her. "This isn't our job. But there's Berardo's name. That's the only reason."

My wife's family lives at San Giuseppe, and we had thought of going there to celebrate the libera-tion of our son, all three of us. That was what saved us.

In fact, we went there and in the afternoon we handed out copies of the paper to the people we met in the street. About nine o'clock, after having eaten some soup and drunk some wine with the relatives, we started out for Fontamara. Halfway there, we heard some noise in the distance.

"What festival is this?" asked my wife, trying to guess what village the sound was coming from.

It was hard to tell what festival it was. San Luigi's had already gone by and Saint Anne's hadn't come yet.

We heard more noise as we went on.

"You might think it came from Fontamara," I observed.

Just at that moment, a carter from Manaforno came by, going in the direction of Fossa.

"Are you from Fontamara?" he yelled at us without stopping. "There's a war at Fontamara!"

We kept going.

"War? Why is there a war?" we asked ourselves. "A war among the people of Fontamara? Impossible!" we told ourselves.

"The Trader's war against Fontamara? Again? But why?"

Every once in a while the noise stopped, but it always started up again more strongly. As we went on, we realized that it came from Fontamara and that it was rifle fire.

"What can we do?" we asked ourselves, thoroughly alarmed.

(It was Scarpone's question: *What Can We Do?*)

But the answer was harder than the question.

Meanwhile we kept on going.

At the fork between the road going to Fossa and the one going to Fontamara, we ran into Pasquale Cipolla.

"Where are you going? To Fontamara? You're crazy!" yelled Cipolla, and he set out toward Fossa.

We ran after him.

"But what's happening at Fontamara?" I yelled at Cipolla. "Why is there all this shooting?"

"War! War!" answered Cipolla. "War against the peasants, against the paper!"

"And what are the others doing?" I asked.

"Whoever could, saved himself. Whoever could, escaped," answered Cipolla without stopping.

"Did Scarpone escape?" asked my son.

"Peace on his soul!" answered Cipolla, crossing himself.

"Did Venerdì Santo get away?"

"Peace on his soul!" answered Cipolla, crossing himself again.

"And Pilato?" I asked.

"He went into the mountains."

"And Michele Zompa?"

"He went into the mountains."

"And General Baldissera?"

"Peace on his soul!"

"And who else is dead?"

From far away we heard hoofbeats coming toward us. It might have been the policemen from Pescina coming to Fontamara.

We threw ourselves into the middle of the fields. In the darkness we lost sight of Pasquale Cipolla.

We never heard of him again.

Nor did we hear anything of anyone else—not of those who died, nor of those who escaped, nor of our house, nor of our land.

And now we're here.

With the help of the Solitary Stranger, we've come abroad. But obviously we can't stay here.

What can we do?

After so much suffering, so many tears, and so many wounds, so much hate, injustice, and desperation—

WHAT CAN WE DO?